I Need A GANGSTA

To Love Me Better

2

D1715598

A NOVEL BY

TREASURE MALIAN

PREVIOUSLY...

Quest

I honestly thought that shit between Aubri and I was going to change after finding out that Lia could possibly be having my baby, but it didn't. Maybe because I was honest with both Lia and Aubri about my intentions from the moment I found out. I was with Aubri, wanted to be with her, and wasn't going to leave her regardless of what the results turned out to be. Of course, I would do what needed to be done for my seed, if that turned out to be the case, but that's as far as it would have gone with Lia. Maybe we were able to look past it because we weren't at that bridge yet. Aubri's energy went into preparing us both for her brother's wedding. It was nice to see her attempting to have a relationship with him, even though I was far from team Curtis. At the end of the day, all she had was me, and while that would always be enough, I liked seeing the side of her that was happy to have a sense of family back in her life. I hadn't been to many weddings; in fact, the only one I did attend was Cross's, but here I was, for her.

It was becoming hard to ignore the heat I felt radiating on the left side of my cheek. Slowly, I turned my head in her direction to find her sitting there staring at me with a smirk on her face. Even after all this time, I couldn't read her mind. For the most part, I could usually tell what she was feeling, or the type of mood she was in, but her face was still unreadable. That's because she could have a smirk or smile while going the fuck off on someone, or have a blank stare while having a cool conversation.

"Why you staring at me like that?" I asked while sliding over in my seat some.

Most of the wedding attendees were either not present yet, or up on their feet mixing and mingling, so the seats beside me were empty. We were super early; I don't know why, when Aubri claimed she didn't even want to come. Not only did she shut her brother's fiancée down when asked to be in the wedding, but she told them she wasn't coming. However, here we were. She went back and forth about coming since she told him yes, ended up telling him no a few times, but again, here we were.

"I can't look at my boyfriend?" she questioned.

Nodding, I reached out and rubbed the side of her face.

"Of course you can, beautiful."

She blushed and leaned her cheek into my hand.

"Thank you for coming with me, Quest."

She had already thanked me a few times, but I guess she didn't think the first five times were enough.

"Aubri, I'd do anything for you."

She leaned back and twisted her lips up. "Is that right? Anything?"

Sliding back closer to her, I leaned over to her ear and whispered, "Anything. Because I'm in love with you."

Aubri blushed and turned her head in the other direction. Reaching over toward her, I placed two fingers under her chin and turned her head back toward me. I leaned toward her while smiling. She moved closer until our lips met.

"Hey, Aubri. You're needed in the dressing room."

I felt Aubri sigh against me while our lips were still touching. Hesitantly, she pulled away from me.

"Cheer up. I'll walk you back there. I gotta make a phone call anyway."

She reached for my hand and stood up while pulling me up with her. She followed the chick who came to get her out of the room the ceremony was going to be held in, and I followed behind her.

"Aubri, remember what I said," I called after her once she and shorty got to the room they were going in.

"Quest. I love you too."

"Oh, you…"

Nah. I had to be bugging. I looked behind me then back to the person who appeared in the doorway. Yeah, I was bugging. Had to be. But to be sure, I took steps in their direction. The expression she wore on her face was stuck between shock and embarrassment. I hadn't seen her in months, but there she was in the flesh, in a fucking wedding dress.

"Quest." Her voiced cracked as I approached where she stood in the doorway with Aubri and the other chick standing in front of her.

"Oh. How you know my future sister-in-law?" Aubri smiled looking from her to me.

Words escaped me, and I just stood there shaking my head.

"He's my son."

"She's my mother," we responded at the same time.

Aubri's eyes bucked, and she took a few steps back.

"Fuck are you doing, Kourtney?" I roared and rushed over to where she stood.

Aubri quickly jumped between us.

"Calm down, please," she pleaded with me.

Yeah, I heard her, but I wasn't seeing her. All I saw was red. All those years of me longing for Kourtney to be a parent. Waiting for her to realize that she was the only mother I had and needed. As a young kid, I didn't want anything more than I wanted my mom. My grandmother tried to fill the void she knew I felt by lacing me with the latest everything, but the void was always there. As a grown ass man, the void is still there; I'm just better at dealing with it.

"Nah, ain't no calm down, Aub. This bitch turned her back on me the minute I came out of her washed up ass pussy, but now she wants to have a fucking happily ever after."

"It's not the time or the place, Quest."

"Fuck your time and your place, Kourtney. When the fuck was the time and place for you to be a mother? I'm glad you doing better for Mason, though."

"You're Mason's mother?" Aubri butted in. I looked at her for an explanation. "That's my nephew," she continued.

"This shit is crazy. You see, I get why you didn't tell me you were getting married. Whatever. But your own moms? How fucked up are you? She did you a solid and raised me, but you gonna take away her chance to see her only child get married. Selfish ass bitch."

"I'm not gonna be too many more of your bitches, Quest."

"Kourtney, honestly, what are you going to do to me?"

"I'm going to get Curtis," some other hoe said, not minding her fucking business.

"Don't." Aubri grabbed her arm. "We'll leave." She looked up at me. "Come on, babe, let's just go. Please."

"I hope your nigga know how much of a gold-digging hoe you are," I spat before turning to walk away.

As my head turned around, it came in contact with a fist. Shit caught me off guard and made me stumble backwards. I caught myself and swung on dude; he stumbled back too.

"Fuck you think you talking to?" he barked, charging toward me.

Aubri jumped between us and caught a blow that was meant for me. She fell back into my arms, gripping the side of her face.

"Sis, I'm sorry yo," he spoke, hovering over us as I assessed the damage to her face.

That one hit caused discoloration on the right side of her face.

"Move your hand so I can see, Aubri." Although I had a good look at it, she was doing her best to shield it from everyone else.

"Can we just go?" she cried into my chest.

"Yeah, we out."

"You gonna pick some bitch ass nigga over your own brother?"

Slowly, I went to reach for my waist. Aubri, already knowing what it was, put her hand on top of mine and shook her head no.

"Please. I just want to leave. Curtis, what the hell is wrong with you? You just find more ways to ruin my life. How the fuck are you going to marry his mother? Did you know who he was this whole time?"

"His mother? Yo, Kourtney, fuck is she talking about?"

"Quest." Aubri pulled my arm, tugging me toward the exit.

Hesitantly, I followed behind her.

"Were you really going to shoot my brother?" she asked once we were outside.

Aubri

I stopped walking and turned to look at Quest. He stared back at me in silence. The throbbing on the side of my face mixed with the headache that came from a mixture of finding out Kourtney was Quest's mom, and the blow that my brother gave me to the face. I was irate and could have probably shot Curtis myself, but part of me needed to know if Quest really would have done it.

"Honestly?"

I nodded, partially already knowing the answer because of the way he responded.

"Yeah, I would have shot him. I wouldn't have killed him, though; he's still your brother. But let me explain something to you. No nigga walking this earth will ever put their hands on me and it goes unpunished, I don't care who they are. And they definitely won't put hands on you."

"Well, that was an accident. He didn't mean to hit me; that was for you."

"So what? If he wasn't trying to be a fucking hero, he wouldn't have accidentally hit you. But yo, I know that's your brother and shit, so if you want to stay for his wedding, you can. I'm out, though. Not supporting anything dealing with that bitch."

Quest walked away.

"So, you just gonna walk away from me?" I called after him. "Quest,

I'm talking to you! Stop!"

He stopped walking and gave me a chance to catch up with him.

"What, Aubri?" he barked, shocking me.

I stepped back and looked at him oddly.

"Why are you yelling at me?"

He laughed and ran his fingers through his beard.

"How this supposed to work? Your brother is marrying my moms, Aub."

"And? So that's it? Fifteen minutes ago, you were in love with me, now you asking me how this supposed to work?"

No response.

"Quest, I'm speaking to you."

He was looking past me.

"Yo, you know her?" He pointed behind me, causing me to turn around.

"I…" My words were stuck in my throat. My heart pounded against my chest and the throbbing in my head intensified. I stepped back and came in contact with Quest's chest. She took steps in our direction. The smile she once wore turned into a frown. It had to be because of the reaction I gave her. I didn't want to scare her, I didn't want her to walk away, but I was shocked. Pain ached in the pit of my stomach, and my heart broke. She took a step back.

"Don't leave," I spoke just above a whisper.

She stopped mid-stride and proceeded to come in my direction.

How did she find me? Here, out of all places. What was she doing here? Did something happen? Did she run away?

All these questions ran through my head, but nothing, absolutely nothing came out of my mouth.

"Hi." She smiled once she was in front of Quest and me.

I wanted to hide behind him. But I spent years in hiding. She was here, in my face. I couldn't hide anymore.

"I'm..."

Finally, I was able to speak.

"I know who you are, Milani."

My heart was so full of love, but I didn't know how to express what I felt. I didn't think I had the right to feel how I felt. I gave away that right, thirteen years ago. Not that I had much of a choice.

"I really do look like you."

She did. From her beady brown eyes, to her narrow nose. Everything about her features screamed me when I was thirteen years old. She just had a lot more body than I did at that age. I completely forgot Quest was standing behind me until he stepped to the side and moved beside me. Milani looked over at him and reached her hand out to shake his.

"Hey, sir. I'm Milani."

"What's up. Quest, nice to meet you, kid."

Looking from Milani to Quest, panic crept its way to the surface. What was I supposed to say to him? How was I supposed to explain it?

"Quest, Milani is my daughter."

CHAPTER ONE

Aubri

*M*ilani looked as if she was more worried about Quest's reaction than I was. Her mouth was shaped in an 'O' and she looked between the two of us nervously. Me? I was frozen. Afraid. Scared even. I played the tough role. I got great at pretending I didn't need or want anyone, but I wanted and needed Quest. My revelation was enough to end us, especially when he was already questioning our relationship because of Curtis and Kourtney. To my surprise, he didn't say anything. Instead, he turned and walked away.

"Quest," I called after him. I spun on my heels to follow behind him and took a step forward, but stopped.

I had walked away from Milani once before. As badly as I wanted Quest to hear me out, I couldn't bring myself to walk away from her again. My heart broke as I watched his back get further away from my sight, but there was another pressing issue I had to deal with.

"Milani." I sighed, turning back to face her.

"I'm sorry. I just—I don't know. Look, I'll leave." She stumbled over her words while looking down at her hands.

Walking over to her, I reached out and placed my hand on hers to stop her from fidgeting.

"Don't apologize. I'm glad you're here. I must ask how did you get here? Does your parents know?"

"Nah, my mother doesn't know. I go to this college bound program over here on the weekend, and I saw that you tagged this location on your Instagram and just felt like it was time to meet you. I didn't mean to just pop up; I just felt like it was right."

"I'm glad you came. We have to call your parents, though. Before anything." I couldn't even wrap my head around the fact that she followed me on Instagram and I had no idea. In addition to that, she saw me posing for ads for work. Not the way I wanted her to know me when we finally had this moment.

"I just really wanted to meet you, Au, mo—Aubri?"

Nodding, I let her know that Aubri was fine. I hadn't been a mother to her, so I didn't do anything to earn that title. "Aubri is good, Milani. Whatever you're comfortable with is good with me."

So many thoughts raced through my head. There was the crazy shit that went down between Kourtney and Quest, and her. Milani was right here in the flesh. My daughter. My baby girl, who was far from a baby.

Without thinking, I reached out and rubbed the side of her face. She was beautiful. Everything a woman would hope for their daughter to be.

12

"I'm sorry." I quickly snatched my hand away after seeing her body tense. "I can take you home."

"Why did you give me up?" she asked. Her tone was harsh, but her expression was soft. Something else she must have inherited from me. I didn't expect her to jump into the deep stuff so soon. I wanted to ease our way into that discussion. I didn't want to have it standing on the street.

"Milani, let's call your parents first. Then I can take you home and if it's okay with them, we can sit and have this discussion. I don't want to have it right here."

"Yeah, that's cool." She sighed while pulling her phone out of her pocket.

My nerves were getting the best of me as I stood watching her punch stuff into her phone. When she placed it to her ear, I thought my heart was going to pound out of my chest and land on the ground beside my feet.

"Hey, Ma. Hold on."

Milani reached her hand in my direction and waited for me to take the phone from her grasp. I was hesitant at first, but knew I had to take it.

"Hello," I spoke while pressing the phone against my ear.

"Hi, who am I speaking to? Is everything okay with Milani?"

"Stephanie, it's Aubri."

"What? How? What happened?"

"I'm bringing her home now. We can talk then?"

"Yes, of course. See you soon."

After hanging up with Stephanie, I handed Milani her phone back.

"Let's catch a cab to your house," I told her before stepping closer to the sidewalk and waving my arm to catch a cab.

Milani stood away from me until a cab pulled curbside. I opened the back door and held it until she slid in, and slid in after her.

"Madison, between Marcy and Nostrand," she told the cab driver.

I looked over at her to find her staring out the window. I'm sure she had a million questions, and she deserved answers.

"Was that you calling me?"

It was a random question, but it had hit me that it was a possibility that she was the random caller. At this point, it made sense.

"Yeah. Every time I thought I knew what I wanted to say, but when you answered, the words escaped me."

"I understand."

"Do you really? Unless you were going through boxes unpacking right after you moved to a new city, to find adoption papers, I don't think you do."

Definitely my kid. The way her attitude switched up on me, had me written all over it. I wanted to tell her the circumstances surrounding her adoption, but it wasn't my place. If her parents didn't feel the need to tell her, who was I?

"Do you know who my father is?" she asked, once she realized I wasn't going to answer her previous question.

Did I? I wish I could forget.

"Okay, if you aren't going to talk to me… Just, never mind."

I placed my hand on her leg and she scooted away from me.

"Milani, I will tell you everything. I just need to speak to your parents first."

"Why? So y'all can get y'all lies in order?"

Shaking my head, I sank a little in my seat. At only twenty-five, I wasn't fit to be dealing with the emotions of a teenager; even if, technically, she was mine to deal with. I pulled out my phone and headed to the text messages.

Quest, I really need you right now; more than ever. If you show up, I can explain everything. Please, just give me that chance. Meet me at 244 Madison St.

After putting my phone back into my bag, I shifted my position and turned slightly toward Milani. Seeing the evident pain in her eyes made my heart break. I knew hurt all too well. And even at thirteen, I thought I was making a decision that would save her from the years of heartbreak I bore and still bore to that very moment. I didn't want to fail her, even though back then it was more about me than it was her. As I got older, I realized the decision I made at such a young age was for the best. At least at the moment it was.

The cab came to a slow stop on the corner of Madison and Nostrand.

"How much is it?" I questioned while digging for my wallet.

He looked back over his shoulder. "Twenty."

After handing him the bill, I pushed open the door and stepped out. I looked back to find Milani emerging as well. After slamming the door, I waited for the cab to pull off before walking over to where Milani was waiting on the curb. Just as I was about to say something, my phone started vibrating. Pulling it out of my bag, I saw that it was a text message from Quest.

Quest Love: * *I'm here, yo. Where you at?*

I looked up the block and spotted Quest leaning against his car, in front of Milani's building.

"You knew my address?" Milani asked as we walked up the block toward the building. I knew a lot about Milani. More than she knew. At thirteen, I knew nothing about open versus closed adoptions, but the family I gave Milani to insisted that we went with an open adoption. Due to my circumstances, they figured that a time might come when I wanted to be in her life, and they wanted me to. To my surprise, that time did come. I was eighteen, and no, I wasn't ready to be a mother, but I knew I wanted to know her. I reached out to her parents, who at the time were still living in Philadelphia. From there, they sent me pictures and kept me abreast of all that went on with Milani, until I was ready to meet her myself. I couldn't do much for her, but when I started dancing, I sent her family money, monthly. They never asked and had a hard time accepting it at first, but they understood that I wanted to do my part for my daughter. Apparently, she didn't need anything, but they promised to keep the money in a savings and give it all to her when she was eighteen, to do as she pleased.

"Yes," was all I said. "Quest, thanks for coming," I spoke once we reached him. He nodded and pushed himself up from against his car. He looked at Milani oddly, then me before shaking his head. "Well, we're going to go inside and speak to her parents."

"Heard you," he said. "Milani, right?" He diverted his attention to her. She looked back while using her key to open the door.

"Yes."

"How old are you?" Quest asked as we walked through the door of the building.

"I'm thirteen."

"Thirteen?" he repeated while looking at me.

We walked down the hallway of the first floor, bypassing the staircase. The closer we got to her apartment door, the more nervous I became. There was a nagging feeling in the pit of my stomach that I just couldn't shake. I've spoken to Stephanie a plethora of times, but this was different.

"Milani!" Stephanie shrieked as Milani walked through the front door with Quest and I on her heels. "What happened? Hi, Aubri. Who's this? What's going on?"

"Mom," Milani started to explain. "I showed up to where she was. I just wanted to meet her."

"But how did you…?"

"I found the adoption papers when we were unpacking."

The look on Stephanie's face was a look of shock and disbelief. We had planned to one day tell her the truth, but this wasn't the way either of us imagined it. I knew how I felt, and it was a horrible feeling. That feeling had to be ten times worse for Stephanie, the woman who had raised and cared for her, for thirteen years.

"Stephanie, look. If this isn't the time, you can call me and we can come back."

Milani shifted her weight to one side and folded her arms across her chest.

"You said you would give me answers. Both of you owe me that much."

While I knew that Milani was right, the more I thought about digging up the past and laying it all out for her, the more I felt the urge to run and not look back. Stephanie was pacing the floor mumbling something beneath her breath. Her brows were furrowed, expression was pained.

"We could wait for your father," I insisted.

Stephanie's pacing ceased. She looked to me then to Milani. "He died," she spoke just above a whisper.

"I'm so sorry." In an instant, my heart broke even more. Milani's life was shaping up to bear more heartache than I wanted for her. She lost a parent and found out she was adopted. That alone is enough to send a person over the edge, but all she wanted was answers. We did owe that to her.

Stephanie walked over to where Milani stood and pulled her in for a hug.

"I just wanted to protect you." Her words were low and genuine. The tone she used was that of a mother consoling and protecting her baby. The things I could say would change that and I didn't want it to.

"Milani, I am so happy you reached out to me. I get that you may want to know me, but Stephanie is your mom. She loves you dearly. Nothing I say will change the fact that she's been everything you needed for your entire life."

"Whether you tell me what I want to know or not, nothing will change the fact that I know you are my biological mother. So..."

Stephanie's head shot in Milani's direction.

"Your tone," she scolded her.

"It's okay. She's hurt. She feels lied to and betrayed and a ton of other horrible things. I get that. Stephanie, if it's okay with you, I'll tell her."

Stephanie gawked at Milani with a thoughtful expression. She had to be making a pros and cons list in her head because I was doing the same. Would it have been bad for me to walk away, leaving Milani to wonder about where she came from, or would me doing that be just as damaging as me telling my story?

"Okay," Stephanie whispered while taking a seat on the chair near the window.

I took a few strides around the living room, taking in the various photos that hung around the room. Milani looked happy in all of them. Not the 'I have to smile for this picture even though I'm miserable' type of happy. She looked genuinely happy; they all did. Slowly turning around, I came face to face with Milani's questioning expression. A few steps in her direction was all it took for me to lose my nerve.

"I can't. I'm sorry. Quest, come on."

I rushed toward the door and left. Behind me, I could hear Quest apologizing before his footsteps caught up to me. He reached out and grabbed my arm, stopping me, just as I made it to his car.

"Why you running? That's your seed, son. All she's asking you for is answers. You gonna walk away?"

In my heart, I knew Quest would be the last person to understand why I couldn't give Milani what she wanted, and it had everything to do with his relationship with his own mother. At that point, I didn't even want to explain to him, let alone relive that part of my life to Milani.

"Answer me. You really want to walk away from the chance to get to know your kid? I can't even believe you have a child, but it's not even about me; it's about her. Imagine how she feels right now. You basically just said fuck her."

"Fuck her? Are you serious, man? I gave her life. I was raped, over and over and fucking over again. But when I found out I was pregnant, instead of killing her like I was advised to do, I gave her life. Me! At thirteen. So don't tell me about how she may feel. Imagine how I feel, Quest. I knew nothing about life or responsibility at thirteen, but I made the decision to bring her into this world."

The pain I'd been harboring for thirteen years was at the surface, threatening to spill over and fill the space between me and Quest. Struggling to keep my breakdown at bay, I looked to the left and right of me, as if I was looking for an escape route. I was. I didn't want to face my reality. I didn't want to relive my past.

"Milani, I'm sorry." Quest reached out for me, causing me to jump back.

Looking down at his hand as if it was diseased, I placed a hand over my mouth. That gesture was supposed to stop the scream from falling out, but it didn't. A slow inhale, which should have been followed by an exhale, was instead followed by a slow shriek. I shuddered and then it happened. Thirteen years of built-up pain and anger spilled onto the sidewalk. Agony was evident in my tone as I stood in the middle of the street wailing. Quest was stumped. His expression was puzzled. I knew it was because he didn't know what to say or do to assist me in the condition I was in.

"I can't breathe. It hurts so bad," I cried.

Finally, Quest moved in my direction. Hesitantly, he reached for me, afraid of how I would react to him. Pulling me into him, he wrapped his arms around me and held me tightly.

"Let me go." I squirmed beneath him.

Quest

*A*ll the confusion and anger I felt after the shit that went down at the wedding and finding out about Milani's seed, was gone. Seeing her breaking down, feeling her shake in my arms, had me ready to kill the nigga who violated her, if he wasn't dead already. And if he was, I would kill anybody who shared his blood. All the pussy in the world, as many bitches who give it up for free or for the low, and you wanna force yourself on a thirteen-year-old. Nigga didn't deserve to breathe.

"Please, just let me go." Aubri pounded against my chest, but I wasn't letting her go.

Everybody she encountered in life had failed her miserably. I wasn't about to add myself to that list.

"You gotta chill, Aubs. You gonna have a panic attack. Just breathe. Slowly," I instructed her while taking slow deep breaths, hoping she'd follow suit.

With my arms still wrapped around her, I side stepped a few feet toward my car. As bad as I wanted her to go kick it with Milani and her moms, she wasn't in any condition to do so. Taking her home was best, at least for the moment.

"Come on, Aubri." I shuffled her around the car to the passenger side, and opened the door for her.

Once she was inside, I walked over to the driver's side and climbed in. I didn't want to make the wrong move. While I thought taking her home was the right thing to do, only she really knew what she needed in that moment. I looked over to her; her head was resting against the window and tears cascaded freely down her cheeks.

"Aubs, what you want to do? What you need from me?" I asked.

She slowly turned her head in my direction while sniffling back tears. "Take me home," she croaked while gazing past me at Milani's building. I turned to see what she was looking at, to find Milani staring at us from the doorway.

"Aight, hold on," I told Aubri while climbing out of the car.

I made my way over to Milani and pulled her in for a hug. Surprisingly, she didn't push me away or anything.

"I know you don't know me, but I give you my word she'll be back. And she'll tell you everything you want to know. You probably feel you don't deserve her understanding, but trust me, we'll all get through this. Aight?"

"Are you my father?" she asked as I broke our hug.

Slowly, I shook my head no. "Nah, but I love your mother, Aubri. So, I'm here for you too. Give me a few days tops and I'll have her back here."

"You sure?"

"Yeah, I am."

She looked around me at Aubri in the car.

"Can I say bye to her?"

I looked back at Aubs then to Milani. Shrugging, I figured there was no harm in letting her have a real goodbye instead of letting Aubri just walk away from her like she meant nothing.

"Yeah. Come on."

We took a few steps away from the building before Milani stopped suddenly.

"It's okay, Mr. Quest. I'll just see you if she decides to come back."

"Just Quest is cool, and we'll be back, Milani."

She didn't say anything else; instead, she turned and headed back into her building. I rejoined Aubri in the car and pulled off. Silence filled the car for the entire ride back to my house. Both of us were too busy with our own thoughts to speak or to worry about turning on the radio.

"I wanna go home," Aubri spoke after fifteen minutes of complete silence.

My eyes were glued to the road. It hurt too much to look at her. The look of defeat mixed with fear and pain that I saw in her eyes, fucked with me.

"That's where we going."

"My apartment, Quest."

"No."

Wasn't about to leave her on her own to deal with what she was going through. We still had the Curtis and Kourtney shit to talk about, but honestly, it was fuck them; right then, it was about Aubri and whatever she needed.

"I don't want to talk about it," she stated.

"Did I ask you to talk about it? I don't care if we lay in bed and stare at the ceiling. I'm not taking you to your crib to be alone."

She knew what I said was final because she didn't bother saying anything else. Instead, she slouched in her seat and leaned her head back against the window. We were nearing my crib when my phone sounded off, alerting me that I had a call. I glanced down at the dashboard and saw that it was Cross. Wasn't really in the mood to chop it up, but I answered anyway.

"What's good?" I questioned, while navigating through afternoon traffic.

"What up? How was the wedding?"

There was a brief pause before I figured out how I wanted to respond to his question. "A story for another day."

"Heard it. You trying to link up today?"

If it wasn't about business, Cross and I hadn't spent much leisure time together. I wasn't still holding the Lia shit against him, but I couldn't ignore the fact that it changed things between us. I still loved him like a brother, but now, I was second guessing him in ways I'd never done in all our years of knowing each other. I didn't like the feeling at all, so I kept a little distance. I did miss my brother though. Glancing over at Aubri only reminded me that she needed me. Unless it pertained to business, Cross had to take a raincheck.

"Today not even a good day, bro."

I didn't know Aubri peeped me staring at her, but hearing her suck her teeth told me that she did.

"I'm not a child. Nor am I fragile. I promise I won't break if you leave me alone," she spat. "Go hang out."

"Bad time? What's good, Aubri?" Cross stifled back a chuckle. I knew he found the way Aubri spazzed funny; if only he knew the half.

"Hey, Cross. And no. He'll call you to meet up once he drops me off."

"Yo, Cross, Aubri just chatting. We'll link tomorrow, bro."

"Aight, just hit my line later."

"Say less," I told him, before ending the call. "You taking your attitude out on the wrong nigga. I'm just trying to be here for you. You really want to be left alone?"

She didn't say anything in response to what I said, so when traffic allowed me to, I slid over a lane and into the first empty parking spot.

"I'm talking to you. Do you really want to be left alone, Aubri?"

She turned her head in my direction and stared at me.

"No. But you're going to leave anyway. Save me the heartache and just end it now."

"Fuck are you talking about? If I wanted to leave, I wouldn't even have shown up at shorty's crib after finding out you had a thirteen-year-old. Only thing I want to do right now, is kill the nigga who thought it was okay to violate you. That's honestly the only thing on my mind right now. Aside from getting you in the right space to get to know your seed. That dead-beat mom shit is—"

"I'm not a dead-beat mom. I'm not a mom. You don't know shit."

"Correction. I know everything about mothers walking away from their responsibilities. At thirteen, you made the right choice by giving her to people who could take care of her the way you couldn't, but you a whole ass grown woman right now. She showed up, and here you are faced with another decision; you not thirteen anymore, fam."

She looked at me blankly. At that point, I dead ass just wanted to shake her until she understood the words that were coming out of my mouth. Don't get me wrong, I sympathize with what she experienced. I can't imagine how she even managed to get through it, but she did. I needed Aubri to remember how strong she was. It was the only way she was going to be able to move forward.

"You made it this far, Aubri."

"Barely," she mumbled. "Just take me home. You can go out with Cross, I just need some time to get my thoughts together. Tomorrow, you can pick me up and we can go back to Milani's."

"How about I take you to my crib, like I said. But I'll go to link with Cross and give you space. And that definitely sounds like a plan for tomorrow."

"Fine, Quest."

I smiled at her while shifting the car into drive. We were finally getting somewhere. There indeed was a light at the end of the tunnel. I honestly didn't want to see Cross because I knew he was going to have questions. Talking about Curtis and Kourtney was the furthest thing from my mind, but I told Aubri I'd give her space, so I was going to stick to that.

Cross

"Glad you called and decided to come through, nigga." I greeted Quest as I opened the door, letting him inside.

He gave me a weak dap and headed toward the living room. Shrugging it off, I followed behind him. I knew things with Quest and I were going to take a minute to get back to the way they were, so I wasn't even stressing the fact that he didn't greet me the way he normally would.

"What's good with you? You want something to drink?"

He looked up from where he had his head down, looking at his phone, and shook his head no.

"I'm straight. I'm still shocked sis let your ass stay here since she and Aubri got back from their little trip."

"Me too." I agreed with him while taking a seat beside him on the couch. "So, you going to tell me about the wedding or nah?"

"Honestly, I don't even know if that shit happened. I mean, Aubs and I showed up and shit was good. But then we found out the bitch her brother marrying is Kourtney."

I perched up from my slouching position.

"Kourtney, Kourtney?" I questioned, only half believing what he was saying.

"Yeah. My moms. Shit went left; after that, Aubri and I dipped, then… Too much shit on my brain today."

"That's fucking crazy though. How old is her brother? Or is your moms into young niggas," I smirked.

"Get fucked up, Cross."

"I'm fucking with you." I guess it was too soon for those types of jokes. "Shit is crazy though."

"While I'm here, I've been meaning to tell you I ran into Lia. Apparently, she's pregnant." Quest said that shit like it didn't bother him or wouldn't affect what he had going on with his shorty.

"Oh word? That's crazy. How Aubri feel about that?" For a minute, I felt bad for Quest. He was getting hit with bullshit left and right. First I fucked up, then finding out his moms is marrying Aubri's brother, and now Lia's news.

"I mean, we haven't really spoke about it. Lia not even sure which one of us is the father."

"What you mean one of us? I don't have no parts in that." Lia wasn't about to have me singing 'when it rains it pours.' I just got to a good space with Ashlynn. Something like this could ruin us for good.

Quest shifted in his seat while running his hands over his head. He looked over at me, shaking his head.

"I mean, you smashed, didn't you?"

"Yeah, but…"

"No buts. You smashed, I smashed, that's simple math, bro."

The fact that Quest was speaking about this situation like it was some minor issue. A baby was a big fucking deal. A little more than simple math. To me at least. See, Quest had it easy. If the baby was his, nine times out of ten, Aubri wasn't going to leave him over some shit that happened before they were together. Ashlynn… My fucking wife? There's no way she was staying around to be constantly reminded of how I fucked up. I couldn't even expect her to.

Quest shrugged me off. I wasn't about to focus too much on that conversation because fathering a kid with someone other than Ashlynn just wasn't in the cards for me. Couldn't and just wouldn't happen. I believed God had a sense of humor, but he wasn't going to do me like that. Well, Ashlynn.

"Besides all that, what's up with Julio?"

"Haven't really chopped it up with him. I told you, a lot been going on. When he call though, we ready."

"Are we? You ain't run no plans by me or none of that, so how we ready? How we moving?" It wasn't like Quest to just expect me to follow behind him blindly without filling me in. If he thought that's how we were gonna move because of the Lia shit, he needed to say that so we could clear that up. Yeah, I fucked up in the personal department, but I never did no fuck shit when it came to the business, so he wasn't going to cut me out slowly but surely.

"Cross, did I ever not come through?"

"Nah, but—"

"Aight then. If I told you we good and I have shit in motion, trust that."

All I could say was, "Heard you."

"Where CJ?" Quest asked, shifting the course of the conversation.

"He was at my mom's crib. Ashlynn went to pick him up a little before you came."

"Gotta spend some time with my little homie. Take him to a game or some shit."

Well that was good, hearing that Quest didn't have plans on letting what was going on between us affect the relationship he built with my son.

"Tryna get ya ass bust in 2k?"

Quest looked down at his watch then back up at me.

"Nah. I gotta shake. Just wanted to touch bases with you."

Looking at him oddly, I opened my arms in a gesture that was silently asking him what's up? He knew what it was too; I didn't need to say a word.

"We good. Just got shit to do."

"So, we lying now, bro?"

"Cross, I'm grown. Fuck I need to lie to you for. You just feeling guilty 'cause you know you fucked up. But I'm straight on you and this situation. No need for us to keep bringing it up or referring to it. I'll hit you when I hear something from Julio."

Sighing, I slid back on the couch. His tone told me where his head was at, even though the words didn't come out of his mouth. Normally, I would stand up and give the nigga a brotherly hug, but I didn't. Reaching up from where I sat, he met my hand halfway, and we dapped before he made his way toward the front door.

31

"Ash, what's good? Ceeeej, I was just asking about you."

Quest bumped into Ashlynn and CJ on his way out. That's when I stood up and made my way to the front door too.

"Hey, bro."

"Uncle Q. Where you been?" CJ wrapped his arms around Quest, giving him a hug.

Q laughed and playfully roughed up CJ's curly fro.

"Been a little busy, Ceej. But I got you next week. We gonna do something, aight?"

CJ nodded before heading over to me and giving me a hug.

"Hey, Dad."

"Wassup, champ."

Quest left and Ashlynn walked in the house. I waited for her to close the door, expecting her to greet me. Even if she just said hi and kept it moving, but she said nothing. This had been the routine since we've been back in the house together. We'd pass each other by like strangers and only spoke if it pertained to CJ, which was rare because he's at the age where he can come to either of us for whatever it was he needed. The stranger in my house feeling was weird as shit, but it was nothing I could do about it.

"Ashlynn," I called behind her.

Nothing.

"Ashlynn!" This time I added a little bass. She stopped mid-way up the stairs, and turned around. Grabbing onto the banister, she looked over at me without saying a word. For a minute, we stared at each other.

I thought I knew what I wanted to say, but I didn't and when she realized that, she rolled her eyes and continued her way up the stairs. I didn't know how much longer I was going to be able to live like this with my wife. One of these days, something would have to give.

CHAPTER TWO

Aubri

The entire ride to Stephanie's house was in silence. I didn't want to hear music, and I most definitely didn't want to talk to Quest about how I was feeling. Silently, I dealt with my emotions. Silently, I cried, and silently, I wished that this day hadn't come. When we pulled up to Stephanie's block and Quest found parking, we sat still in silence. I glared out the window as rain beat down on his car. It was as if the weather was an omen for the somber mood I was in. I should have been ecstatic. I should have felt nothing but joy. Instead, I felt pain and agony. It had nothing to do with Milani but everything to do with the demons I was battling. I hated that my daughter had to pay for the sins of her parents. I prayed for the day that I would be able to sit down with her, face to face, to tell my truth, but now that, that day had arrived, I just wasn't ready.

"You ready?" Quest asked, pulling me away from my own thoughts.

In that moment, I wished he could read minds so that he would have already known the answer to that question before asking.

"I'm not," I told him honestly.

He reached over to me and rubbed my arm.

"That's fine, Aubs. But I'm right here. I will be right here no matter how it goes in there. I honestly think this is what's needed for the both you. Her to hear the truth, and you to release a burden you've been carrying around for thirteen years. It's a win-win. Will it hurt? Yes, I'm sure it will. But it won't hurt any more than how much it will hurt if you walk away and have to keep wondering what would have happened if you were honest with her, or still walking around with this same guilt."

He was right. I couldn't begin to imagine continuing with my life carrying this burden, especially now that I had Milani in my life. I turned to Quest, looking him in the eye, searching for a sign that told me he was bluffing. Part of me wanted so bad to believe that he wouldn't stay, that he wouldn't be able to understand my truth. Believing that he wouldn't be able to deal with it, would save me from the heartache I thought would follow once he knew everything. People didn't stick around for me. That was a known fact. As bad as I wanted Quest to be the exception, history taught me that everyone in my life was a part of the rule. They all left.

"So come on, Aubs. Let's get inside and deal with this head on. You got this," Quest asserted while getting out of the car. He didn't even bother to let me respond to him. Instead, stood on the side of the curb in the rain, waiting.

Although hesitant, I ended up pushing open the door and emerging after him. Not before grabbing my umbrella from the back seat though. The walk to Stephanie's building was dreadful. My hand shook while trying to hold my umbrella steady. All I could think about was how things could go wrong. I knew I should have been thinking of a positive outcome, but positivity was the furthest thing from my mind when this whole situation stemmed from torment. As we reached the door, the urge to turn and run back to the car intensified, but I stood firm. Reaching forward, I pressed the buzzer and waited for the buzz, alerting us that we were being let in. Quest opened the door and held it open as I walked into the building. The beating of my heart could be felt against my chest cavity and grew stronger the closer I got to their apartment. Before I could knock, Stephanie opened the door and greeted me with a surprising but welcoming hug.

"I'm happy you decided to come back." She smiled while letting us in.

I stepped into the apartment and my eyes immediately scanned the room for Milani. I slowly exhaled, releasing the breath I didn't even realize I was holding.

"She's in her room," Stephanie assured me after seeing me sigh in relief.

I nodded uneasily before making my way further into the living room.

"I really am glad you decided to come back, Aubri. I've had a lot of time to think on it, and I think this will be good for Milani. For you as well."

"What about you?" I countered.

I know how I felt about meeting Milani and possibly being a part of her life, but I couldn't begin to imagine how that would feel for

Stephanie. She was her mother. She raised her and nurtured her in ways that I wouldn't have been able to. How will it be for her having me back in the picture? A constant reminder that the child you took care of isn't biologically yours? How would she feel if Milani and I started to build a relationship? There were so many moving factors in this situation, and trying to come up with the different ways things could turn out was exhausting.

"I owe you everything, Aubri, you know that. Raising Milani hasn't been easy in the least bit, but if I had to do it again, I would. Hopefully, the circumstances would be different, but you understand what I'm saying, right?"

I nodded but grew silent. I didn't want to think, let alone speak about the circumstances surrounding Milani's adoption, but I knew eventually I would have to.

"Well, I'm not going to talk you to death. You can go back there and talk to her. She's ready to know you and where she comes from. She's mature, and I'm pretty sure she can handle it."

I moved closer to Stephanie and reached out for her. She opened her arms and pulled me close.

"Thank you for taking care of her, Stephanie."

"It's the least I could have done for you, Aubri. Believe me, I wish I could have done more."

I stepped back to look into Stephanie's eyes. She was sincere. Although there was more she could have done for me, I understood, now as an adult, that her back was against the wall. She couldn't do everything, but the most important thing, providing a life for Milani, she did. And for that, I'll always be thankful, no matter what.

"Why didn't you tell me about Richard's passing?" I asked, switching the topic from me going to speak to Milani, to her not telling me.

"Well… No need for us to talk about that. Go see Milani. I'll keep this stud muffin company."

I looked back at Quest, who was blushing at her calling him a stud muffin. If Stephanie wasn't in her late fifties, I would have decked him from smiling so hard. I was stalling. Wasn't really looking forward to the much-needed conversation I was about to have with Milani, but I knew it would be best if I got it over with.

"Her room is the first door on the right," Stephanie spoke while pointing down the hall.

After looking back at Quest and getting a reassuring head nod from him, I turned and headed in the direction she had pointed. The door to Milani's bedroom was open, but I didn't want to just barge in; instead, I tapped lightly on the doorframe, gaining her attention.

"Hi. Come in," Milani spoke before reverting her attention back to the iPad that was resting on her lap.

She was sitting in the center of her bed, with her legs folded, Indian style.

"How are you?" My attempt to converse failed because she whispered fine and shrugged me off.

An awkward silence filled the space around us. I stood idly, staring at her and allowing my eyes to dart around her room. Typical teenage room; very girly, lots of pink, stuffed animals, and of course, essentials. In addition to that, I found that she was accomplished. There were numerous medals, trophies, and certificates placed around the room.

"Track?" I questioned while raising one of the gold medals and examining it.

"Yes. I run the 3000-meter steeplechase, and 1600-meter relay." For the first time since meeting her, I heard some excitement in her voice.

"Ahh, you must be good. You have so many awards for track. You still run since you moved here?"

Finally, she placed the iPad down beside her and climbed off her bed. After slipping her feet into the fur slides that were beside her bed, she walked over to where I was standing, examining the awards on her shelf.

"Yes. I run, dance, and I made the cheerleading squad while maintaining a ninety-five average."

To say I was impressed would have been an understatement. In that moment, I felt like a proud mom, even though I had no hand in helping shape her into the young woman she was becoming.

The footsteps approaching caught both of our attention. Milani and I turned just in time to see Quest posting up outside of her room.

"What's up, Milani?"

"Hey."

"Not barging in on y'all; just wanted to make sure the both of you were good. I'm not going to pretend to understand what either of you are going through, but I'm here for whatever. For both of y'all."

Milani chuckled and sat down at her computer desk.

"Thanks for that, Quest, but she isn't telling me anything. Instead, she wants to talk about track and—"

"I was raped, Milani. At twelve, I was raped and gave birth to you at thirteen. My parents were dead, I had no family who cared enough about me to care for you." I paused and stared at Milani, who had spun around in her desk chair and was staring back at me intently. She looked as if she was holding her breath, anticipating what I would say next.

Quest sensed my uneasiness and placed his hand on my shoulder. I reached up to where his hand rested and rubbed it. My heart was aching, and the feeling in the pit of my stomach was agonizing; yet, having him there made it a little less painful.

"I couldn't do anything for you at thirteen, Milani. I couldn't do for myself. I couch surfed from home to home. Ate leftovers from fast food spots when they were closing. Slept in train station at times. The thought of being somebody's mother was unfathomable. And not because I was raped; because even still, I loved you. I found out I was pregnant when I was three months and loved you as much as a twelve-year-old knew how to love. That wouldn't have been enough love to raise you how you needed and deserved to be raised." My voice cracked, and I cleared it right before tears sprang from the crevices of my eyes.

Before I lost my nerve, I went on to explain the years of emptiness

I felt after giving her up. The years of regret and feeling as if I failed her, when in all actuality, I myself was the one who was failed.

"I'm sorry you were raped. I can't imagine what that was like for you. My thing is, you didn't look back. You claimed that you loved me, how you longed for me, and was full of regret, but you never looked back. Here you are, seemingly doing well for yourself, but you never looked back for the person you claimed to love and the person who would have loved you back."

"Well for myself? Milani, you don't know half of the life I endured. Until I met him, I stripped and worked at BJ's. I live in a shitty ass apartment, where I struggled majority of the time because the money I did make, went to care for my dying grandmother. I have no fancy degree or accomplishments, so exactly what could I have offered you?"

Milani sprang to her feet and shouted, "A mother! You could have saved me the heartache of finding out the way I did. You think I care that you dance? I knew that the moment I started following you on Instagram. I just wanted to know you. The person who brought me into this world! But it's clear you didn't want the same."

Stunned was what I was. I couldn't begin to respond to what she said because I felt her pain. As I got older, I never thought that me being her biological mother would be enough for her. I had the belief that when I showed up, I had to have something tangible, something that would make her proud to say that I was her mother. Never in a million years did I think just being Aubri was enough.

"She isn't to blame for how this all came out, Milani." With tear stained cheeks and one hand pressed against her chest, Stephanie walked into the room.

She stopped between Milani and I, who were inches away from each other. I looked back at Quest to find him erasing proof of a lone tear. He gave me a weak smile in an attempt to comfort me.

"Don't defend her, Mom!" Milani screamed.

"Listen to me. Aubri wanted there to be a time where she could get to meet you, and your father and I were one hundred percent here for that. You cannot fault her for wanting to be the best version of herself before she met you. She cares about you, Milani. If she didn't, I wouldn't have you. She's sent you money that we've been banking and promised to give to you at eighteen. She called, she texted, she remembered every birthday, and sent a present, making us promise to say it was from us. Christmas as well. When you bruised your ribs playing softball, she flew to P.A. to make sure you were okay. She did what was best. If you want to blame anybody, blame me."

I gasped, knowing where Stephanie was taking the conversation. I didn't think she would want me to get that deep into things, but here she was about to lay it all on the table.

"Milani, Aubri was raped by my…"

I had to force myself to tune her out so that I wouldn't break down. I was here for telling Milani the truth, but now that it was unfolding before my eyes, I wasn't ready. Turning toward Quest, with a look on my face that told him I wanted to make a break for it, caused him to move closer to me. He placed his arms on my shoulders and spun me around, silently telling me to face it all.

"Your son?" I caught the tail end of what Milani said in response to Stephanie, as I brought myself back to the moment.

Stephanie was in tears as she continued to explain in words I couldn't find. I was indeed raped by Stephanie's son. No one believed me until I popped up pregnant, and even then, there was an ongoing battle about how to deal with it. I had no one in my corner to speak up for me. At the time, I was supposed to be living with my grandmother, but she was getting sick, so coming back to the city to find a way to make money was my only option. I didn't care that I had to sacrifice a roof over my head to make money, because if I didn't find a way to care for my grandmother, she wouldn't have had a roof over her head either. These were the challenges I faced at twelve.

"That nigga in jail, right?" Quest blurted out with disdain oozing from his tone.

Stephanie looked over at him with saddened eyes and shook her head no.

"I know you wouldn't understand or agree with me, but I couldn't send my son to prison. He was sick and needed help. A correctional facility wouldn't have helped him any."

Quest's eyes shot to me as my body shuddered. All I saw in my head was the memory of Stephanie and her husband coercing me not to press charges. Of course, now at the age I am, I knew that I should have gone through with the charges, regardless if people would have believed me or not. I didn't deserve what he did to me, and he deserved to go to jail. However, they said all the right things at the right time.

"Since the day Aubri gave birth, he was shipped away and was never allowed to return. If he did, his father and I told him we would turn him in," Steph told Quest.

His nose flared as he raised his hand to pinch the bridge of it.

"And you thought that was enough?" His tone was above normal, which meant he was on the verge of spazzing out. I had to intervene.

Gently pushing him against his chest, I pushed him back and whispered, "It's okay, Quest. Let's just go."

He stepped around me, disregarding my plea.

"Nah, it's not okay. So it went from your son raping her, to you sending him away, and getting custody of her seed?"

"It wasn't like that," Stephanie objected.

Quest wasn't letting up. "So what was it like?" He paused and looked over at Milani. He wanted answers and understanding, but he knew who the full out truth would hurt the most, and although she wasn't his seed or even a friend, he cared about Milani's feelings because he knew I cared. "Milani, you want me to drop it?"

Without raising her head from staring down at her hands in her lap, Milani shook her head no. "I want to know," she stated.

"Yeah, me too."

"Aubri had a choice, Quest."

"A choice? I was thirteen years old. What choice did I have? Send her into the system that would nine times out of ten fail her? You and your husband told me you would take care of her, and raise her right, love her. And while part of me didn't want to believe that because you raised that monster you call a son, I didn't have a choice. Giving Milani to you was my only option, and fortunately, you kept your word. She's happy and healthy, but believe me, Stephanie, I didn't have a choice."

"So, you knew Aubri's situation and you basically used that to your advantage to save your son. You could have at least taken her in too, for all that."

"I tried. My husband wouldn't allow it. The deal was for Milani, that's it."

"The deal? Two lives are ruined behind this shit, and you call it a deal?"

Milani jumped up from her feet and rushed over toward the door, before she was stopped by Quest.

"I don't want to hear any more. I don't want to be here. I can't think. I… I can't breathe." Her chest heaved in and out before she broke down into sobs. "She's my grandmother. Aubri left me here with the family who raised her rapist. What if they would have taken him back? What if he would have done the same to me?"

Her questions were valid, but again, at thirteen, I wasn't thinking about that, although I should have. All I heard was, she'll be taken care of and that was good enough for me, then.

"I really just want to get out of here," Milani wept.

"Aight, grab a jacket and we can go for a ride to get some air." Quest looked at Stephanie, but didn't ask her permission. It was like he was daring her to object.

"That's fine. I'm sorry, Milani."

Milani ignored her, grabbed her jacket that hung on the hook next to her bed, and stormed out with Quest on her heels.

Quest

*W*asn't even able to pull away from the curb, before I was interrupted by the ringing of my phone. I thought about ignoring it so that Milani could have my attention, but when I saw it was Julio calling, I had to answer. Quickly, I tapped the speaker button on the steering wheel.

"Hold on," I instructed. Didn't want Julio saying some shit while I had the phone on speaker.

Glancing over my shoulder, I slid over into the left lane and went straight for another block before coming up on a parking spot.

"Give me a minute, Milani."

After taking the phone off speaker, I leaned back in my seat with the phone pressed to my ear.

"What's good?"

"You busy?" That was shocking coming from Julio. Nigga normally didn't give a fuck if you were busy or not. When he called, he expected you to drop everything you had going on to tend to what he needed you to tend to. I guess now that I meant more to him, I was gonna get better treatment.

"Nah, not really. What happened?"

Last time I spoke to Julio, he assured me that he was getting shit together for me and Cross. I hope this call was to tell me that everything was in motion. The way he pressed us to step up, you would have thought everything was already in order.

"It's go time. Material will be here in a week. Won't know the exact day until the day before, so just be ready. Have a plan in place for how you will take care of everything."

Nigga thought we were gonna take on all this work and not have a plan to get it off. Who the fuck he thought he was dealing with? But now that he mentioned it, I made a mental note to get up with Quavo about the said plan.

"We got that under control."

"Good. So I'll be seeing you in the next week."

"That's it?"

"Yeah, unless you have some concerns."

I looked over at Milani before answering his question. "Nah. All good on my end."

I hesitated because my situation changed from when I accepted the offer to level up in his organization. I didn't know where this shit with Milani and Aubri was headed, how much time she would need, or none of that. What I did know though was that I had to be here for her. At the same time, I had to take care of business.

"Yeah. Everything good. See you in a week," I spoke before ending the call. Me repeating that everything was good, had everything to do with me convincing myself versus him.

"Where we going?" Milani asked as I leaned forward in preparation to check my mirror before sliding out of the parking spot.

"Wherever you want to go."

She was quiet for a moment before slowly exhaling air that I didn't know she was holding in.

"Can I ask you a question?"

Nodding, I shifted my body in her direction and waited.

"Would you forgive her?"

Why did she have to ask that out of everything? Aubri was my girl, and no matter what, I was on her side. But at the same time, I didn't want to lie to her. She had been lied to enough. Plus, I wasn't that nigga. Always shot my shit straight; wasn't going to change that today.

"Honestly, no. Well, not today. Eventually, yeah."

"See, I don't know if I ever can. I want to, Quest. She's my mom. Of course I want to know her and have a relationship with her. But she left me in the care of people who allowed their son to get away with rape. How could she?"

Milani's point was valid. That shit threw me for a loop too, but then I had to remind myself that this was a thirteen-year-old girl who had nothing. Maybe Milani needed to be reminded of that too.

"She was thirteen, Milani. I'm not excusing that decision in the least bit because you're right. But I can't ignore the fact that she had nothing or no one. What options did she really have? And I'm not telling you this because I want you to forgive her. I do. But I want it to be on your time and your terms. Both of you need to heal before moving forward."

She turned away from me, slouched back in her seat, and stared out the window. Proceeding, as I was before she stopped me, I pulled out after checking the mirrors.

"You can take me home. When we get there, take her away. I don't think I want to know her."

It wasn't my place to debate her on that. All I could do was hope that one day she changed her mind for both of their sakes. The ride back to Stephanie's crib was awkward. I could sense that Milani didn't know how I felt about what she said, so she was uneasy. It was a weird ass ride for me because I knew I had to be the one to tell Aubri that she didn't want to be bothered with her, and I knew just how much that was going to affect her.

"Thanks for taking me to get some air."

Before I could respond, Milani was out of the door and on the sidewalk. I watched as she walked to her building before pulling out my phone and texting Aubri to come outside. After fifteen minutes of waiting, I decided to head in to see what was the hold up. Just as I stepped up on the curb, Aubri came rushing out of the building with arms folded across her chest, sobbing. I rushed to her side and pulled her into me.

"She told me she never wants to see me again. It wasn't supposed to be like this."

Definitely wasn't. I expected Milani to let me break that to Aubri; I would have done it gently.

"She just needs time. You both do. I promise you, it's gonna be aight, Aubs."

We shuffled toward the car. My arms were still wrapped around her. Only time I removed them was to open the car door and help her inside. She wouldn't look at me, but I knew she was crying due to her low sniffles. There was nothing I could say that would take her pain away in that moment. It was a process, and all I could do was be there along the way.

CHAPTER THREE

Ashlynn

*W*eeks of pretending that one another didn't exist. Weeks of not being touched by the man who had the power to ignite my soul. The way I was longing for Cross was crazy. The sad part is that it was strictly sexual. It killed me that I just wanted to feel him inside me versus just resting my head on his chest and talking about our day. But this is what our relationship had been reduced to.

Hearing him walk up and down the hallway only made me want him more. I think he knew what he was doing. I had just come back in the room I once shared with him after getting a glass of water, and that's when he chose to keep walking past the room. He was begging for my attention, and I needed attention from him. I guess that moment was the best time to help each other out.

"Cross," I called out with my head wedged between the bedroom door and the frame.

He stopped just as he reached the other end of the hallway. Slowly, he turned to face me. He probably expected me to say never mind and retreat into the bedroom, but I had other plans. He was in for a surprise.

"What happened?" he asked.

Raising my hand, I summoned him to me. The walk he took down the hall seemed to last forever. I was anticipating what was going to happen when he reached me. Once he did, I didn't bother voicing what I wanted. Instead, I pressed my lips against his and pulled him into the room. He already knew what it was, what I wanted, and he was going to give it to me.

My husband pushed me on the bed and I allowed him to. It had been a while since he had been between these legs, and I just needed this. Not him or our marriage; sex. It was the only thing that had been constant in our marriage, the one thing that didn't go wrong between us. My legs had a mind of their own as they spread for him. As I turned my head away from the sloppy kiss he went to place on my lips, I eyed my clothes sprawled on the floor next to his. The sun had just risen in its complete glory. He came in two hours ago, but that didn't stop me from getting him into our bedroom instead of letting him get some sleep. It used to be ours; as of lately, I felt like it was just my room. Like we were two ships passing in the night, or more like roommates who didn't share a son or a marriage together. I used the word roommates loosely. Cross stayed down the hall in the guest bedroom, and came to the room we once shared to shower and get dressed since it's where all his things were.

Cross rubbed my pussy with his thumb and got me wet, which wasn't hard to do. Even though he had betrayed me, he was still a fine man. One thing I prided myself in, was still being attracted to my husband after all these years. His touch didn't electrify my body like it usually did. Cross could set sparks off with my body, and today he wasn't. Quickly pushing his hands away, I pulled him down and flipped on top of him. Shoving his dick inside of me, I rode him slow, trying my hardest to get into the rhythm we had perfected over the years. It was gone. Lost. Not there. As much as he held my hips and pumped inside of me, I couldn't find it.

Flashing back to the night of our wedding, I recapped the whole night as I rode him quick. With my eyes squeezed closed, I recalled how slow and passionate we were that night. Soon as I opened my eyes, the feelings disappeared. I was left to stare at this man that broke our vows and our trust. He broke it literally in pieces, and I had to pretend to be whole in front of our son. With my eyes closed and head pointed up to the ceiling, I slapped my pussy down on his dick hard and grabbed ahold of the headboard.

"Shit, baby, you making me feel good," he groaned as he slapped my ass.

Although I hadn't opened my eyes, I closed my eyes tighter and continued to ride him. In my mind, we were up to the part where he licked me from head to toe on our wedding night. The way his tongue flickered across my pearl was enough for me to cum. With one hand on the headboard and the other resting on his chest, I squeezed my muscles together and continued to bounce on him like a trampoline. The vision of Cross kissing me on my neck and telling me how much he loved me caused me to cum all over him. He tried to hold on to me to let him get off, but I pulled away from him and laid beside him.

Pulling the covers up to my chest, he looked at me confused.

"You can go back to the guest room now," I told him, and he looked at me like I had lost my mind.

"You dead ass?"

When I didn't grant him a response, he sucked his teeth while climbing out of the bed. I lied there motionless, wishing him away because I didn't want to argue. I was wrong, but what he did was ten times worse. The least he could do was help me nut when I needed it.

Upon hearing the door close behind Cross, I released the breath I was holding. Completely spent, I lied there inhaling and exhaling until my breathing was normal. Guilt riddled my body. Deep down, I knew having sex with Cross was leading him on. I had no intentions on going there with him, but I did. And felt absolutely nothing afterward. As horrible as all that may sound, I was hoping that some type of feelings came back. I was tired of moving on autopilot and living in an empty marriage. I would even say loveless, but that would be going too far. Bullshit aside, I still wholeheartedly loved him, just couldn't stand his black ass. However, I said I would give us a chance to make it right, and I was sticking to that.

Turning over in the bed, I buried my face into the pillow. What I needed was time away again. I just couldn't bring myself to ask Cross to leave when I was the one who invited him back home to begin with. Maybe I could take another trip out of town. As quick as that thought came, it left. The one person I wouldn't mind going away with hadn't even returned my call in like a week. I wondered what had Aubri so preoccupied that she couldn't shoot me a text.

"Oh, I know how to reach you, chick," I said out loud while reaching for my phone on the nightstand.

After waiting for my phone to recognize my fingerprint, I went straight to my contacts and called Quest.

"What's good, sis?" He answered on the first ring, so I was assuming his phone was in his hand already.

"Hey, what you doing?"

Shuffling could be heard on his end.

"Shit, just finished eating breakfast and shit. You? You good? Cross straight?

"Relax. We're both fine. I actually wanted to see how Aubri was. She hasn't been answering my calls or returning my text messages."

"Oh, so fuck me, huh?"

While laughing, I pulled myself up in the bed.

"Nah, it's not like that. Just wanted to check on my girl, that's all."

Quest sighed.

"What happened? Where is she?"

"She gotta tell you, Ashy. And she's upstairs."

Now, I was really concerned.

"Well, can I come over?"

"I mean she probably... Matter fact, yeah. Pull up. That just might be what she needs. Plus, I really gotta dip out on her today. Been neglecting shit I had to do to stay cooped up in the crib with her. I won't feel so bad about leaving if you're with her."

"What's going on that you can't leave her alone? I'll get it out of her. I'm about to shower and get dressed. I'll be over there soon."

"Aight, sis. See you when you touch down."

Something told me to take the day off, and I'm glad I did. Apparently, I was needed elsewhere. It took me a minute to catch my bearings before I decided to get up and greet my day. First thing first, was handling my hygiene.

Aubri

"Get up." Quest's voice roared just as he ripped the covers back from clinging to my naked frame.

I rolled over, while sucking my teeth. "I don't want to get up, Quest."

"This sulking shit is wack. I gave you some time to be upset and shit, but that's a dub now. Ashlynn on her way over here so y'all can go get your nails and shit done or whatever."

I heard what he was saying, but I wasn't really trying to hear him. Quest couldn't possibly understand how it felt hearing Milani tell me that she didn't want me in her life, and she wished she never approached me the day of the wedding. That shit hurt because through everything that I've endured in life, the one good thing I looked forward to was having her back in my life and having some type of healthy relationship with her. Now that, that was out the window, my one glimmer of hope for a decent life moving forward was dim. I had Quest and knew he would do whatever necessary for me to be happy, but it wasn't enough. Nothing would be enough. She was my kid, and when the time was right, I wanted to be there for her.

"Who asked you to call her?" I snapped. Ashlynn was my girl, but I wasn't ready to face her. I knew that when I did, I would have to talk to her about why I've been dodging her calls and invites to meet up. I wasn't ready to reveal that part of my life to anyone else.

"Fuck you mean? I don't need a reason to call my sis. And I didn't even have to call her. She hit me, checking on your ass. But, like I said, she on her way so get up, Aubri. I gotta go out and get to it, but I'll hit your phone. Don't be in the crib when I do."

He didn't give me a chance to object or argue, because when I turned over to face him, I was met by his back as he walked out of the bedroom. A few minutes passed before I decided to pull myself out of bed and face the day. As I sat on the edge of the bed, I turned to the left and my eyes landed on my phone that was on the nightstand. I thought about calling Milani, just to let her know that I wasn't giving up on being in her life, but decided against it. I needed my energy for the day out with Ashlynn.

A half hour and a hot shower later, I found myself standing in my and Quest's walk-in closet, sifting through clothes. I don't remember when so much of my things ended up in his closet, but I had so many options to choose from. I settled for a pair of ripped jeans and an oversized sweater from Yeezy Season 2. It was going to go good with the tall boots I planned on wearing. I had just slipped into my jeans and had nothing covering my top when someone rang the doorbell. I knew it was Ashlynn, so I grabbed my robe and headed downstairs to let her in.

"So, it takes Quest to make seeing you possible? What I do to you, Aub?" Ashlynn spoke while pushing past me and making her way into the house.

"You didn't do anything to me. I just been going through it, that's all. Let me put on a top and we can be on our way."

"Wait, wait, wait a minute. Wait one damn minute. We not going anywhere with the sour puss ass attitude you got going on. Let's chat."

She reached for my arm and pulled me toward the living room. I stood stoically, as she sat on the couch and crossed one of her legs over the other.

"So, what's going on? Quest fucking up?"

I shook my head no.

"How are things with you and Cross? How has it been being back home? We haven't really had the chance to speak about it."

Ashlynn shifted in her seat and rolled her eyes.

"Let's not make this about me, Aub. But Cross and I are okay, I guess. We're working on it. But forreal, what's going on with you? You look different, and I don't mean it in a 'you loss or gained weight,' 'changed your hair color or style' type of way. There's no life in your eyes. You know you can talk to me about whatever."

"I have a thirteen-year-old daughter," I revealed while taking a seat beside her.

Ashlynn's mouth nearly hit the carpet at my revelation. She didn't speak though; instead, she allowed me to have the floor completely. I went on to explain everything that happened to me back then, and how Milani ended up back in my life now. Somewhere between telling her how Milani basically casted me out of her life and trying to express how much I needed her to be better, I ended up in Ashlynn's arms, crying.

"I'm so sorry you had to go through that, Aubs. I can't imagine what life has been like for you," she whispered into my head as I wept on her shoulder. "I wish you would have come to me sooner about this. I would have been there for you. I'm sorry."

"It's like the minute I think things are going to start looking up for me, life reminds me that I'm not meant to be happy."

"You can't possibly believe that. You have to give your daughter a chance to digest this. You feel how hard it is for you, so you have to know that it's hard for her as well. Her life as she knew it has been pulled from beneath her feet. Time heals wounds, my love. Just let her know that you're here for her now, and you won't go away again. When she's ready, she'll reach out."

Part of me knew that Ashlynn was right. But an even bigger part of me couldn't comprehend what she was saying because I was too full of guilt and pain. I tried to reason with my subconscious by continuously telling myself that I was thirteen. Thirteen! Faced with an impossible decision.

"Thank you, Ashy. I'm gonna put on my sweater and we can go." I forced back the tears that wanted to continue to flow.

I was cried out. I spent the past few days crying, and both Quest and Ashlynn were right. I had to shake the pity party. I was going to take her advice and reach out to Milani to let her know that I was here and would always be here. In the meantime, I was going to focus on continuously bettering myself and my relationship with Quest, if there was still going to be a relationship once we faced the fact that his mother and my brother were possibly married. Another issue we swept under the rug as if it didn't exist, when in fact it was very real.

"Aubri!" Ash called after me.

I stopped at the bottom of the steps and turned toward her.

"I'm okay, Ashlynn. I promise." My attempt to assure her that I was okay, was weak because I only half believed it myself. In that moment, I was tired of being strong; well, at least pretending to be strong. I wanted to be weak, but I knew with everything I had going on, being weak wasn't an option. Finding strength from somewhere, I pushed forward, taking the steps two at a time. Once I was back in Quest's room, I grabbed my sweater and pulled it over my head. Grabbing the bag I had sitting on the dresser, I headed back out the room to meet Ashlynn downstairs.

"So, where to first?" I asked once I joined her in the living room.

She stood to her feet and walked over to me.

"Before anything, we going take care of this little mop on your head, chick." She playfully tugged on the messy bun that rested on top of my head.

We laughed while heading toward the door.

"Yeah, I can definitely go for a wash and set, and somebody's nail salon," I admitted.

"That's what we'll do then. A little pampering and then grab brunch. We gotta hit a spot with unlimited mimosas."

"You driving?"

Ashlynn waited for me to face her after locking the door before responding.

"Every time we step out, I gotta drive. What if I wanted to get shitfaced?"

"Shit, I need to get shitfaced so, Uber?"

She laughed while pulling out her phone. I guess we agreed that we both needed a few drinks and would have to depend on Uber to get us from point A to B.

"It says two minutes," she announced as we made our way down the driveway.

Inhaling deeply, I took in the fresh air. I was feeling real Nina Simone-ish, *new dawn, new day*. Wouldn't say I was feeling good, but for the first time in days, I felt like things would be okay. It's amazing what wonders fresh air could do for a person.

"Thank you."

Ashlynn looked over toward me and smiled.

"For what? Letting you know that your hair looks a mess. You're welcome. That's what sisters are for."

Together, we laughed. A real genuine laugh.

Ashlynn

After what Aubri revealed to me, seeing her smile and hearing her laugh really put me in a good place. Honestly, I couldn't imagine all that shit happening to me at that age; and even more so, I couldn't imagine getting through it. Aubri was strong, and now that I knew her story, I understood her so much more.

"You not even listening to me," she griped before taking a sip from her Bellini glass.

"I am, pooh. My bad, I zoned out for like two seconds."

"What's on your mind?" That's another thing I liked about Aubri; no matter what she had going on, she still cared about what was going on with everyone around her.

"Nope. Not doing that. Today is about you, chicken little."

"I'm good. Forreal. Coming out the house, getting my hair done and shit, got me feeling good. Don't get me wrong, it's in the back of my mind. But I'm good. I know that everything is a process. What could I really expect from her?"

While open to hear her out and lend a shoulder for her to cry on, I had no idea what to say. I wasn't in her shoes and hadn't remotely experienced what she had. What I could offer was my support, and she had that one hundred percent.

"You're right. I'm glad you are smiling though. Just know that for as long as you need, I'll be here until you're one hundred percent in a good space. And even when you get there, I'll be here."

"Excuse me, ma'am. The gentleman over there had me deliver this to you."

The waitress standing beside me took my attention away from Aubri. I looked up to her, to find her holding a bottle of champagne in one hand and pointing toward the bar with her free hand. Glancing, in the direction she pointed, I smiled and mouthed *thank you.*

"How sweet. Can you send it back?" I asked her.

She looked confused. "Are you sure? It's paid for already."

"Yeah, I'm sure. Thank you."

She nodded and spun on her heels to return the bottle. Giving the mystery man another look, I smirked and returned my attention to Aubri.

"Good to know I still got it," I told her before laughing and sipping from my glass.

She nearly choked on her drink before saying, "Well, he's coming over here."

Scoffing, I put the glass down and adjusted my posture. I wanted to come off standoffish but still keep it cute.

"You just going to hurt my feelings like that, huh?" He slid a business card on the table while speaking.

Glancing down at the card, I noticed he was into real estate as well. Slowly, I turned in his direction and raised my head to meet his gaze.

"Didn't mean to hurt your feelings, sir. We're good though. Thank you for the gesture."

For the record, I love my husband. Pissed at him, yes. But at the point where I want to violate the vows I made before God and our family? Absolutely not. But what was the harm in taking the number. At the end of the day, I didn't want to be rude. I don't know If I was saying this to myself to convince myself that I wasn't doing anything wrong, or if I really believed it. The side eye I was getting from Aubri was telling me what she was thinking without her having to say anything. She could judge all she wants; this was my moment, and I was going to enjoy it.

"Please, I insist." He placed the bottle back on the table and tapped the tip of his fingers on the business card. "Gotta get back to the office, but please, use this."

I looked up at him and smirked. He returned the gesture before backing away.

"Well, he was cute." I stated the obvious, while turning back around to face Aubri. "Josh Hamilton." I read the name on the card slowly.

"He's a killer. What kind of black man name is Josh Hamilton? Give me the card, Ashlynn."

Aubri held her hand out and wiggled her fingers so that I could place the card in her palm. Slowly, I slid the card off the table and put it right in my bag, while laughing at her facial expression.

"What? He's in real estate. Who's to say we can't do business together? You know I'm big on networking, Aubri."

She grimaced and shook her head. "Yeah, whatever."

The way she folded her arms across her chest and twisted her lips at me was humorous. She was probably reading me my rights in her head, the way I tried to read her when I thought she was creeping with Quest.

"But when you thought I was dealing with Quest while he was with Lia, you all but lost ya shit. But ya married ass can take this man number because y'all both work with property? Oh, okay."

I really couldn't contain the laugh because she said exactly what I knew she was thinking. What ended my laugh was the fact that she was right. Regardless of how rocky my marriage was, it was still a marriage, and I valued that. If I was to move on with someone else, the ink on Christian and my divorce papers would be dry.

"Aight, you got it, Aubri. Don't claw my damn eyes out."

While sucking my teeth, I removed the card from my bag and handed it to her.

"We can enjoy this champagne though, right?" I joked.

Aubri cracked a smile and held her glass up. She was about to say something, but stopped suddenly when her phone started ringing. I watched as she looked down, rolled her eyes, and tapped the screen, sending the caller to voicemail.

"What's that about?" I inquired.

"My brother," she stated flatly.

There were very few conversations had about this mysterious brother of hers, but by the way her mood just switched up, my interest was piqued.

"What's wrong, Aubri? This is our ladies day out. We can clear the air, vent, cry, whatever is necessary."

She inhaled, rubbed her temple, and took a sip from her glass. As she set it back down on the table, she shifted in her seat.

"I don't know where to start. My brother and I have a rocky past. Without me even getting into all of that, more recently we found out that he was marrying Quest's mom."

"What!" I bellowed, momentarily forgetting where we were. After looking around, making sure people weren't looking at me like I was crazy, I turned back to Aubri for an explanation.

"Yeah. I don't know if they went through with the wedding or whatever, but just the thought is sickening. He's been calling, but I don't have the energy to deal with him. I could probably find the energy to, because at the end of the day, he is my brother, but I just don't want to. I'm probably a shitty person for that."

See, that's where I had to stop her. Holding up my hand, I shook it side to side while shaking my head as well. "Nah. You have every fucking right to protect your peace. It's okay to cut toxic people out of your life, family or not. Don't forget that shit. I don't know the history with you and your brother, but I know if he's not adding to your life; positivity into your life, then him and everything around him is a dub, and that's okay. Protect your fucking peace. You hear me?"

Her legs shook beneath the table. I could tell by the way her body moved slightly.

"Yeah, you're right. I'm just tired, Ash. Between my brother and his shit, Milani coming back into my life, and Lia's pregnancy bomb, I'm tired."

Whoa. The whole Lia pregnancy thing was news to me. Shit really has been piling on thick in Aubri's life. I thought I had it bad, and I did, but my girl was going through it. It's funny that I tried to focus so hard on how Aubri was feeling about Lia being pregnant, but the thought of her baby belonging to Cross still crept into my mind. I had to shake that thought though, because that's most definitely something Cross would have been upfront about, if it was the slightest chance. Plus, it was just one time. I couldn't have done someone that wrong in my past life that, that type of karma would greet me. Yeah, I felt for Aubri because I couldn't imagine having to accept a baby that didn't belong to me. Women do it every day, but usually on their terms. She didn't ask for this.

"Wow. I don't even know what to say to that. You are really having a tough go, Aubs. I'm sorry. You really just need to busy yourself with something that you will do for you, so that bullshit will have less opportunity to consume you. You passed all the real estate courses, so I say you jump into that full time with me. You learned fast, I'm sure you'd be great at it."

"Can I get you ladies anything else?" the waitress approached us and asked.

Aubri glanced down at her empty glass, then back up to the waitress.

"Yes, please. A water with lemon."

I added, "Make that two."

Once the waitress was out of earshot, Aubri cleared her throat in preparation to respond to me.

"Let's make a deal."

Leaning back in my seat, I crossed my legs and smacked my lips. Whenever someone said let's make a deal, some stipulations that the other party would more than likely disagree with, was sure to follow.

"Continue," I insisted.

"I'll go full throttle with working at your company, if you do one small thing for me."

She paused, I guess waiting for me to say something, but I wasn't going to. When she realized that, she went on.

"Make it right with Cross. And before you tell me no, hear me out. We both know you aren't leaving him because you haven't left yet. So, I need you to remember how short life can be. You and Cross don't have perfect, but you most definitely have worth it. Fight for that before it's too late. Not to mention, you guys have CJ. He deserves to grow up in a loving and functional home. Don't take that away from him because you want to make Cross feel the pain you felt. It's not his fault and he shouldn't have to suffer. You made the decision to stay, so be there."

Never being one who had an issue with admitting when someone was right, I had to let her know that she was. I made the decision to stay with Christian when CJ and I went back home, for Aubri's. It was time for me to stop pretending and clear the air with him so that we could move forward.

"Touché, Ms. Aubri. You have a deal. So, I'll see you in the office Monday morning?"

71

"As long as if on Sunday night, you call me to say you had a much-needed conversation with your husband."

The waitress had returned with our waters. I took the glass from her hand before she could place it on the table, and held it up toward Aubri, silently sealing our deal, and she did the same.

Quest

Leaving Aubri wasn't something that I wanted to do, but I had to. My meeting with Julio was approaching and being cooped up with Aubri wasn't going to do shit for me, in terms of making sure I had my ducks in a row. I felt bad for dipping, but not so bad because she was in good hands. I had to link up with Quavo about some shit for Julio. I didn't trust many niggas, but Quavo and Trey, in addition to Cross, I knew would hold it down. It just so happened that I still had Cross on a little time out. Loved my nigga but I needed space.

After leaving the crib, I decided to make a little detour on the way to my meeting with Quavo. Although I spoke to my grandmother on the phone daily, it was nothing like seeing her face to face. A little pop-up visit was overdue. As I pulled up to her crib, all I could hope was that Kourtney wasn't around. After the whole wedding debacle, I wasn't ready to see her ass. More so, I hoped that my grandmother didn't know about the wedding. That shit would kill her knowing her daughter made such a huge step and didn't have the decency to invite her. As I got out my car, I paused and thought that maybe seeing her before my meeting wasn't such a good idea. I wouldn't be able to focus if my grandmother did know about the wedding and expressed to me how she was hurting, but I was already there so I went ahead.

"Beautiful lady," I called out after letting myself in.

Normally, she would get on me for yelling instead of coming to find her, but she didn't respond. The living room was the first place I looked for her, since that's usually where she kicked back in her recliner and caught up on her shows; but she wasn't there. Wasn't in the kitchen or her bedroom either. While heading back to the kitchen for a bottle of water, I called her.

"Hey, there's my favorite guy in the world."

Just hearing her voice alone made my heart smile.

"Grandma, what's up, my love? I called myself surprising you and ended up being the one surprised. You not even home."

"Oh, no. Are you there now?"

I sat at the counter, opened the bottle, and took a sip.

"Yeah. Where you at?" I knew my grandmother had a life. She had a gang of old lady friends who she went shopping with and did cheesy shit like visit art galleries and stuff, so I wasn't too surprised that she wasn't home."

"You remember Carol? The one that lives on the corner of my block?"

While nodding, I told her, "Yeah. You down there?"

"No. Carol scored some tickets to the museum of sex. I'm down here with her and Susan."

"Ma, are you kidding me?"

"What? Your mother wasn't dropped off by a stork, Quest. Sex ain't foreign to me. Boy, please, okay?"

There's no way I was getting into that conversation with my grandmother, so I had to switch the direction of the conversation and fast.

"Aight, aight. Enough with all that. Be safe and call me when you make it home. I'll come back later on."

"If I don't get in too late, I'll make you something to eat. I love you."

"I love you, more."

After hanging up with her, I shot Quavo a text.

Yo, Qua. Where you at?

Placing, my phone on the counter I chilled and drank my water until his reply came through.

Quavo: *I'm on the block. Pull up.*

Sliding off the stool, I tossed the empty bottle into the recycle bin and texted him back as I made my way to the door.

Sayless.

<>

Quavo's block was always popping. It didn't matter the season, or time of day. Everybody found a reason to be outside, and today wasn't any different. When I pulled up to his crib on Georgia Avenue in East New York, I honked to get his attention. The nigga was sitting in front of his crib with a few cats I knew, but didn't care to socialize with. I watched as he dapped up his company, made his way over to my whip, and got in.

"What's good?"

We dapped each other before he pulled a blunt out of his pocket.

"My nigga," I nodded.

Qua and I were on the same type of time 'cause I pulled a pre-rolled L out of my pocket too, and sparked it.

"So, Cross and I made a new move that will be making us more money than we imagined making."

He beamed with excitement.

"You know I'm all for the paper. What's the move?"

While Quavo was a nigga I knew I could trust, there were still some parts of the business that had to stay strictly between me and Cross. That would never change.

"Nothing you gotta worry yourself with. Cross and I got everything under control," I explained to him between pulls on my blunt.

He blew smoke out while nodding. "Y'all ain't never steer me wrong. So, let me know what's needed of me."

"I need to move at least five hundred bricks at one time."

"Nigga, what? Five hundred? You need a fucking boat to get that shit around undetected, Q."

"That would be ideal. For the future, I plan on looking into buying a sea shipping company. But right now, I need something to move that much work. Like, now. I was thinking your cousin…"

"Ahh, yea. Meeko. Trucks is a good idea."

"I knew we'd agree on that. So, you think Meeko would be down to let us use his trucks?"

"You know he always looking to make some money."

"That's what I like to hear. Get up with him and let me know the numbers he talking. I mean whatever it is, I'll pay it, but don't let ya cousin rape me."

Quavo laughed while shaking his head no. "Nah, he ain't on the type of time. Plus, he fucks with you for the shit you did for him a little while back. Don't worry. You can count of the trucks. You gotta secure the routes."

"That's nothing. I know a few people. Just let me run the plan by my guy first and make sure that he thinks it's solid, and we'll be on the move."

"Say less."

"Get up with Meeko, ASAP."

Quavo tossed the clip out the window before rolling it back up. "Soon as we done here, I'ma go get up with him."

See, that's why I knew to come to Quavo. He was about his paper, no bullshitting.

"Aight, let me not hold you up then. Let me know what he says, and once I talk to my guy, I'll get that bread over to you."

"Aight, stay up."

We leaned into each other for a brotherly hug and he got out. Me, I headed back to my crib to rest up for the meeting I had with Julio the next day.

CHAPTER FOUR

Cross

A nigga had never been around so much coke at one time in my fucking life. To say I was excited would have been putting the shit lightly. I wasn't so much excited about being around the product as I was about how much money we were going to rake in, once we got all the work off. Stepping up in Julio's business was looking like an even better idea, each and every day.

"Five hundred bricks of pure cocaine. I assume you guys aren't biting off more than you can chew with taking on this much at once. Or too little? I'm all for pushing the limits as long as the outcome is income," Julio stated, even though he should have known better.

Quest and I have never got off more than a hundred bricks in a shipment. It wasn't because we tried and failed, but because we never wanted to push it. Our hundred-brick cap, kept our business flowing steady with minimal problems. We had a point to prove though. Quest and I had to show Julio that he made the best decision in the interest of his organization, and at the same time, we were going to line our pockets. I don't know what Quest's plans were moving forward, but mine were to get out. Almost losing Ashlynn over the Lia shit only reminded me how important she and my son were to me. I wanted to enjoy the perks of the life I busted my ass to provide for my family, while I could. Too much was going on for me to have that conversation with Quest, but it was coming. Eventually.

"Nah, we got this," Quest assured him.

"Good. I was getting worried. It took you a little longer than expected to get up with me."

Julio's concern was valid because I had the same one. For days, I had been hitting the nigga, Quest, up trying to link and make some money moves. Each time he had a new excuse, one weaker than the last. I figured he was still in his bag over the Lia shit, but nothing usually came before money for him. Unless it had something to do with Aubri. Lately, she's been the most important thing. Not saying that's a bad thing, because I like shorty for him, but the grind should still be important to him.

"Had a lot going on and shit. Wanted to make sure my head was in the right space to get to work. I'm good now."

Julio clapped once and smiled. "Well, that's good to know. What's your plan to move that much work?"

I looked to Quest for the save because I hadn't had the slightest idea how we were going to do it. It was never fucking discussed.

"Aight, so we have an associate we work with. He got a plug with a trucking company. The plan is to put decals of some of the largest delivery companies on the trucks. We have a few people that work with Frito Lay, Domino's, and a few other companies, so getting our hands on their routes and delivery schedules won't be an issue. We send our trucks on their routes with a minor detour to a specified location to unload the product." Quest went on to lay out his plan from top to bottom without missing a beat.

Don't know if I wanted to be proud of the nigga or to feel some type of way because he went on and planned all of this without even running it by me. Last time we linked up, the nigga told me he had some things in motion and that was that. He really was ready to level up, and today he showed me he was willing to do it without me. At the same time, I was relieved. We would have looked like amateurs had we not had a plan.

"Sounds like a fool proof plan. Will your drivers be armed? Where do you guys get your artillery from?" For the first time since we arrived, Jordano decided to speak up.

It was shocking that he showed up to the meeting with his father in the first place. His hating ass thought he was fooling us by playing along with his father's plan for him to tail us, but we knew otherwise. At least I did.

Quest shifted the position he was standing in, turning his back toward Jordano and addressing Julio.

"Where we get our weapons from doesn't matter. The question for you, Julio, is would you rather us get them from you? When we handle our business, I deal with who I deal with but this your operation, let us know."

Julio rubbed his hands together before walking further into the warehouse and gesturing for us to follow them. I lingered back a little and let Jordano go ahead of me before following. Julio led us to a back room that was wall to wall stacked with weapons. From hand guns, to sniper rifles, the room was stocked as if it was the armory for an impending war.

"Continue to get your heat from your people. Just know that if the time comes and you need a little extra, we covered on this end."

Quest nodded.

"Copy," I stated.

"Ay," Julio snapped, remembering something he wanted to say. "I have some guys out in Miami who are looking to get into business with us. I want you two to take a trip down there soon. I haven't decided on the date yet, but soon. Just be ready."

We shot the breeze for a little while longer about other ways we could go about distributing. One thing for certain, I left the spot with a lot more respect for Julio and how he ran his business. Quest and I had done business with niggas who moved like El Chapo, Griselda, and the best of them, and the way Julio was showing shit to us, put him right up there with them. We thought we knew him before. Taking the higher position in his operation was showing us a whole new side. However, no matter how enticing shit was, my plan was still to get out.

"You type quiet," Quest pointed out after we had already been in my car and on the road for like fifteen minutes.

"Yeah, just thinking about some shit. Nothing major." Part of me wanted to end the conversation there, but an even bigger part of me wanted to let the nigga know what was on my mind. "Actually, my nigga. I know I fucked up. More time, you put on this front like we were gonna move forward and shit, but then you keep me out of the loop with important shit. This not how we move. Never should I be in a predicament when I'm completely in the dark about OUR business because you decided to do make moves and decisions without me. Type time you on, Q? Let me know so I can move accordingly."

"You think it's that easy?" His tone was low, but I heard him clearly.

"Nah, I don't. But at the same time, I'm not gonna front like I'm good and putting the shit behind me, when I know I'm not. Keep it a buck. What we need to do for you to get this shit out of your system."

Slowing the car down, I flipped the blinker on and slid into an empty parking spot. After killing the engine, I turned to Quest.

"What's up? You wanna get out and shoot a fair one? What needs to happen for us to move forward if that's what you want to do. In this business, I need to know that I can trust you with my life and vice versa. Not that we going to be making a move and some shit going to happen, leaving me looking dumb 'cause I didn't know that plan."

He was quiet but oddly enough, I could kind of see the wheels turning in his head.

"Start the car back up, nigga." His tone was light, leading me to believe that he wasn't taking me serious.

"Are you fucking hearing me, Q?"

"Nigga, I heard you. Fuck you screaming at like that? I look like CJ? My nigga, I don't need to verbally respond to your ass. So what I left you out of the plans? You know that ain't nothing. I killed niggas for less than what you did to me. We still here. Brothers fight. Get the fuck over it. Let me be mad until I'm not any more, bro. And you know you can fucking trust me with your life or you wouldn't be here right now. Can I say that same?"

My eyes nearly popped out my fucking head. This nigga had to be gone off some Xan or something to say some dumb shit like that to me.

"Yeah, you see how dumb that shit sounded, right? Of course, I know I can trust you with my life, but that don't make you fucking my bitch an easy pill to swallow. Chill out, b."

And just like that, the mood changed. I felt where Quest was coming from and he was right. He had a right to be in his bag over what happened, but even with that, in the back of his mind we were still us.

"Speaking of her, have you heard anything from her?" he asked.

"Niggggga. You really think I want to talk about that chick? Nah, I didn't hear from her and on my son, I hope I never run into shorty or I might break my no putting hands rule on a female and beat the shit out of her. Quest, no more Lia talk, bro."

He laughed at how worked up I got over his question.

"Sensitive ass nigga," he joked. "Take me to the crib. And aight, as long as you stop the whole *why you leaving me out thing*, I'll drop all conversation dealing with Lia."

"Bet."

Lia

Growing up, my parents stressed how bad sex was, in hopes of keeping me from having it. What they should have focused their speech on was getting pregnant. That for sure would have made me keep my legs closed. I'm pretty sure once I give birth, my baby will make it all worth it, but this… the gaining weight, back pain, morning sickness? I was over it. Things probably would have been better if the circumstances surrounding my pregnancy were different. Quest would have without a doubt made this better. He would have been the man he needed to be for me and our unborn baby. But because the paternity of my baby is up in the air, he kept his distance. Couldn't really blame him. The night I seduced Cross, I thought I would be hurting Quest the way he hurt me, but now months later, I see I'm the one who got the short end of the stick. When it came to Quest and Cross, it was truly a 'bros before hoes' situation.

"Ms. Perkins." Hearing my name being called pulled me away from thoughts of my tumultuous pregnancy and baby daddy drama.

Just as I stood to my feet to follow my doctor to the back, my phone started vibrating in my hand. I glanced down to see who it was, but decided against answering, and slipped it into my bag as I approached my doctor.

"How are you, Dr. Sloan?"

"I'm great. How are you? Still have the constant back pain?" He stood aside, holding the door open for me to enter the corridor that led down to the private exam rooms.

"I've done the expecting mom massage a few times at the place you recommended, and it's eased up the pain. The morning sickness, though."

"Ah, if it's not one thing it's another, huh?" he joked.

I chuckled as I helped myself up onto the exam table and got comfortable.

"Yeah, but it will be worth it, right?"

"That's what I've heard."

Dr. Sloan stood over me and helped me lie back on the exam table. After prepping his table, he slipped on gloves and hiked up my shirt.

"So, let's see what we have going on here."

I turned toward the screen as Dr. Sloan put gel on the probe and placed it on my stomach. Maybe I didn't have to wait until after giving birth to see that it was worth it. Hearing her steady, strong heartbeat, warmed my heart and made me smile. I never got enough of ultrasounds. Still couldn't believe that a human was growing inside me, but there she was.

"Looking good. Measurements are as they should be, heartbeat is strong, no signs of any complications thus far. We're doing extremely well."

"Thank you for everything."

I came to Dr. Sloan as a wreck who knew nothing about pregnancy.

I mean, the basics, of course I knew. But this was beyond anything I expected. It was growing on me, though. Literally.

"Nine more weeks. We're almost there."

"Yeah, almost."

I waited for him to wipe the gel off my stomach before pulling my shirt down and sitting up. We spoke a little more about what to expect the next nine weeks, before I set my next appointment and was on my way. As I stepped outside of the doctor's office, my phone rang again. It was the same caller, so I sent him to voicemail again. Only this time it didn't stop at the phone call. Hearing a car honk behind me caused me to turn around, and that's when I saw him parked directly across from my doctor's office. Clearly ignoring him wasn't enough; he just had to show his face. Deciding against pretending as if I didn't see him, I headed over to his car and climbed in the passenger's seat.

"I told you I would come with you. What's your problem, man?" He called himself scolding me.

"And I told you I was fine coming alone. I'm tired of this back and forth. I wish y'all would just let me do what I need to do for me and my baby and when the time comes, I'll involve y'all."

I thought he was going to have a smart remark but all he offered was a laugh.

"I'm not them other niggas, Lia. I don't care if we don't know if the baby is mine yet. I'm willing to be here until we find out. I don't want to miss shit like this then it comes out that she's mine and I regret it."

"If only Quest had that sentiment. He so far up Aubri's ass that..."

Realizing what I slipped up and said caused me to end my sentence abruptly.

"What you just said?" he questioned with one brow raised.

My options were to lie, get out the car and run, or tell the truth. However, the baby brewing inside me only gave me one option at this point, and it was to just tell him the truth. In the event that he did turn out to be her father, the truth would come out anyway.

"Sean, listen to me," I started to explain.

"Nah, repeat what you said, Lia."

"Okay, look, I know Aubri," I admitted.

He gestured his hand for me to continue.

"She's with my ex-boyfriend."

"Did you know I knew her when you pursued me or what?"

I guess I wasn't getting to the point fast enough. But yeah, I did know. How was I supposed to tell him that he was just a part of my plan to hurt her the way she forced Quest to hurt me. Sean was actually a cool guy and was also on my list of regrets and dumb ass decisions. Bringing him into the situation was totally uncalled for, but it was too late.

"Answer me, Lia!" he barked.

"Yes. Yeah, I knew you knew each other. After Quest kicked me out, I did a little homework on her and followed her sometimes. I saw you two together a few times, and the way you looked at her, I knew you meant something to her. I didn't know to what extent until I started to kick it with you and you told me about the one that got away."

"Yeah, in the same conversation that I told you I took dick too when I felt like it."

I slouched back into the seat realizing his point in bringing that up.

"How fucked up are you? You probably never dealt with a bisexual nigga in your life, but because you was hell bent on some revenge because you're bitter, you just went with the shit." Disgust oozed from his tone.

Hearing him say it out loud was worse than the way I heard it in my head.

"This shit is crazy. You're fucking crazy. That little girl gonna need all the help she can get with a mother like you."

"And if you're her father? What, she gonna grow up confused as fuck?"

"If she is, it won't be because of me. I'm not confused. I know what the fuck I am and how I live my life. You need help, dead ass."

"Are you going to tell her?"

He slammed his hand against the steering wheel.

"That's all you care about, Lia? You got way worse problems than worrying about the conversation I may or may not have with my best fucking friend."

A slight smile crept across my face hearing the way his tone changed when he called Aubri his best friend. He did care about her, deeply. This wasn't something he was going to be upfront with her about, because she'd probably never speak to him again. This was going to be between us. At least for a little while longer.

"You're right. If you tell her, Sean, I just have to deal with whatever consequences. We both will. Are you going to take me home or what?"

"All the niggas you sucking and fucking, now you want me to take you home? What about your nigga? Any other time I offer to do something for you, it's your nigga this, your nigga that, now it's cool for me to take you home?"

All I did was nod. Wasn't going to go back and forth with him because for the time being, I still had the upper hand and was very much in control of the situation on all fronts. For a minute, I lost sight of that, but I was. The baby I was carrying kept me out of harm's way from all parties involved, so I was going to use her to my advantage while I could.

"He's out of town. Are you going to take me or not? And I'm starving, Sean."

He sucked his teeth and started up the car.

"Put your seatbelt on," he instructed.

Without hesitation, I reached above my head and pulled the seatbelt down over my protruding belly. From my peripheral, I peeped Sean looking at me with disgust. Unfortunately, I didn't feel like taking the train, so I had to block out his dirty looks until I got home. When we pulled up to my house, I couldn't get out of the car fast enough.

"I'll call you with updates pertaining to the baby," I told him as I got out.

That was a lie. Even if my baby turned out to be his, I wasn't going to tell him. That sucked, but him being a part of the equation was never supposed to be a thing, and if raising her on my own is what I would have to do, then so be it. After wobbling up the driveway to the home where my boyfriend was renting for me, I had to stop to catch my breath. Being pregnant was no joke. All I did was walk a few feet and I was winded. I used that time to dig my keys out of my bag. As I was taking the keys out, my phone started vibrating. Quickly, I answered and pressed the phone against my cheek while letting myself in.

"Hey, bae."

"Yo, let me ask you a question."

Something must have pissed him off, and of course, he was going to take it out on me.

"What happened?" I asked while picking up the mail and looking through it.

His background was noisy at first, but I guess he knew that and started making his way to a quieter area. The noise slowly faded.

"You been playing when it comes to giving me information on Quest. You think I'm dumb? Giving little ass bits and pieces of information when I know you know a lot more."

"Bae, why do you think I know this man's life? Quest didn't tell me shit. He paraded me around when he wanted to and that's as far as it went. I didn't get to socialize with his friends, just a select few. I literally told you everything I knew."

He blew out air. I knew he was getting fed up with me telling him I didn't know anything, but it was the truth. Quest never discussed business with me, and the little I did know was shit I overheard and was never meant to hear.

"What the fuck I'm keeping you around for then? I'm putting you up, making sure you eating, with a crib and shit, and you ain't no fucking help." His voice bellowed, causing me to jump.

"I... I..."

"Quit with the stuttering shit. Tell me something useful or be out my spot by the time I get there."

I really couldn't afford to lose the stability he provided me, so I pondered on what I could tell him.

"One of his boys I can turn. One of them niggas gotta be weak."

That was easy.

Hesitantly, I uttered, "Trey."

"See, was that hard? Text me everything you have on this Trey nigga."

"Okay."

I was about to end the phone call, but the piece of mail in my hand stopped me.

"Bae, did you buy me a car?" I questioned, while staring down at the mail from the Acura dealership. Even after the way he spoke to me, I was excited at the thought of having my own wheels again.

His laugh killed my excitement. "Nah. I got a car in your name but it ain't for you."

I was perplexed. "I'm the pregnant one, and you get a car in my name for you instead of for me."

"Lia, you being knocked up really not my problem," he admitted before hanging up the phone on me.

CHAPTER FIVE

Ashlynn

A few days passed since Aubri and I had our girls' day. Tomorrow was Monday and I wanted to hold up my end of the bargain. Not because I needed her to work for me, but because I knew she needed something else to focus on besides her daughter and the drama with her brother and Quest's mother; I wanted this for her. Since I used Cross as a booty call, he'd been real skeptical around me. I found it a little funny because he was really acting like a female who got dissed by a nigga. If I told him to come to the room for something, he would bring CJ with him. He said he didn't want me to seduce him again. The nigga really felt used. Although I got a kick out of that, Aubri was right. The jig was up.

I heard Cross come in a little while ago, but he never made his way upstairs. Since I was choosing to be the bigger person and initiate a peace treaty, I decided to set out to find him. My house was huge, so I'm glad I didn't have to search high and low. He happened to be in the first place I looked for him, which was the living room. Without saying a word, I took a seat beside him and for a minute, we sat in silence until we said, "we need to talk" in unison.

Nervously, I laughed. For the most part, Cross had said all he needed to say. All his apologies and how badly he wanted to make it work, so he needed to hear me out.

"Me first?"

He nodded.

"I've been a complete woman for as long as I've known you. Because of you, my confidence has been through the roof. My self-esteem was intact, and my heart was fully functional. I've never had to second guess my place in your life. I've never had to second guess myself as a woman. But what you did with Lia, changed all of that, Christian. I loved you beyond my core. You know how my family instilled the bible in me growing up, and yes, I've strayed from being the church-going girl I was growing up, but my principles are still intact. Everything a wife is supposed to be for her husband, I've surpassed that for you, and you've been everything I needed. I've cried for you, went without so that you could have; of course, this is before you were on, but I've been your partner. Never strayed. I kept you whole. When things didn't make sense in your world, I made sense of it for you. I gave you a legacy. And you turned around and broke me. Because of you, I look in the mirror and think am I enough. Because of you, I feel replaceable. My soul aches because of what you did to me. And still I love you. Still I want to be with you. Still I believe together we can conquer the world.

My step always had pep, because in my world, I had everything I could ever ask for. My walk is less peppy, my smile isn't as bright, my tone isn't as assertive. You did that. Still, I love you. I didn't know how to move past what you did, but I knew that I wasn't ready to walk away. I don't want to be an empty shell in search of who I used to be. The woman I was prior to you, I never wanted to meet again. But here I am. So, I'm asking you to fix me. Make me whole, bring back my smile. Rebuild my confidence. Make me believe I'm enough. In my heart of hearts, I believe our marriage is worth it. Trust me, I know it was a mistake. I know you would never intentionally do this to us, but it doesn't change the fact that it happened."

Cross

Ashlynn hadn't seen me cry since the day CJ was born, and before that, I can't even remember. But in that moment, all I could do was cry. I mean, I knew I hurt her, but the pain was so evident in her voice. It's like her aura radiated hurt. Never did I want that for the love of my life. She spoke of all the things she'd done for me, when she'd done even more for me.

"I'm sorry. I've told you that a lot, but I mean that, Ash. You are enough. I gotta do more than tell you that, but you are. There is no woman in the world that can take your place. On CJ. If you were to leave me today, I'd never be a quarter of the man I am with you. I'm so good at everything I do because I know whatever I lack, and if ever I fall short, you got me. I know how blessed I am, Ashy. I fucked up. I'll spend the rest of my life making it right, but I don't want to give up on us. We are worth it. I've never thought otherwise. You and CJ are my world. All the money and all this shit don't mean nothing to me without y'all. If giving it up would mean you'd have your pep back, and your smile would light up every room you walked in, I'd do it in a heartbeat."

Reaching over, I rubbed the side of her face.

"You are the only woman for me. I want to fight whatever battle or war. I'll fight that shit for you. For us. What we have is real, Ashlynn. Not only is it real, it's rare. I'm not perfect at all, but that's an indisputable fact. It shouldn't have happened, and it'll never happen again. I love you too much to ever see you in this space again."

She moved closer to me and leaned her head on my shoulder.

"I just want my best friend back," she whispered.

"Right here is where I'll always be," I told her honestly.

The thing is, I wasn't as good with my words as Ashlynn. The way she expressed how she was feeling to me, I couldn't do that. It had a lot with me never having to do it and being more of a doer. I was well aware that people could talk 'til they were blue in the face, saying all the shit they knew you wanted to hear, but their actions wouldn't match. I was an action guy and she knew that.

"What now?"

I looked down at her, kissed her forehead, and sighed.

"Well, tonight, we can kick back and watch a movie with CJ 'til his bedtime, and just ease back into being who we were before all this shit. A nice little getaway needs to be in the works too."

"Yeah, CJ been asking about Universal. Some time away for us three would be great."

"Yeah, I got a lot to make up to my boy too. No matter what goes on between us, CJ should never see us in dysfunction, ever."

"I agree." She placed her hand on top of mine and rubbed it. "We'll be okay. I'll get on planning the trip for us. And together, we'll get each other back to where we need to be."

"Nothing would make me happier, Ash."

She placed a gentle kiss on my cheek and stood up.

"I'll make sure CJ is bathed and we'll meet you in the room for movie night, okay?"

"Yeah, I'm right behind you."

I watched as Ashlynn made her way out of the living room before reaching for my phone that vibrated on the coffee table.

"What's good, bro?" Quest had bad timing. I hope he wasn't calling me because he needed to link up. Tonight, would have been one of the rare nights where I told him I couldn't make it.

"Nothing, just finished kicking it with Ash. What's good on your end?"

"I won't keep you. Just wanted to let you know the truck situation is a go. Spoke to J and he wants us to make that move south in the next two or three days."

"Good. Good. Shit falling into place. I'ma stay low these next few days 'til the trip. Gonna play home and shit."

"Yeah, do your thing. If anything changes, I'll update you. Give Ash and Ceej my love."

"Will do. Stay up."

"Say less."

After ending the call with Quest, I headed upstairs for the movie. Walking in the room, I found CJ and Ashlynn laying across the bed. I switched into a pair of ball shorts and joined them. It was this very moment, lying with my son between my wife and I, that made every trial I've ever faced in life worth it.

CHAPTER SIX

Aubri

*H*onestly, I had a feeling Ashlynn would be calling me telling me that she had talked with Cross. Maybe I was hoping she did because I really needed to get out the house and out of my own head. With Quest always busy, I had way too much time to myself to think. I needed to be occupied, so I was looking forward to going back and working with Ashlynn full time. I was in the process of ironing some business attire and listening to Chinx, when my phone started ringing. After setting the iron up on the ironing board, I walked over to the dresser and grabbed it. The number wasn't saved in my phone, so I thought to ignore it. Didn't want to risk it being Curtis. He had been calling a lot and probably got tired of me ignoring and him and decided to call from a number I didn't know. Sucking my teeth, I sent the call to voicemail and went to set it back down. Before I could fully let it go, it was ringing again. Frustration set and I gave in.

"Hello," I snapped.

"Hey, Aubri. I know I'm probably the last person you want to hear from."

"Uhh, who is this? If you are calling me on some Barbara this Shirley type stuff, I don't have the time or energy." Had to let that be known. Never would I be the chick beefing over the phone over a nigga, even if it was Quest. I loved him, but if he put me in that situation, Barbara and Shirley could have him.

The caller chuckled. "No, no. This is Kourtney."

"Kour—Kourtney?" I stumbled, only half believing that she was really on the other end of my phone.

"Yes. I just…"

Curtis really had me fucked up, making his cougar ass wife call me. "No disrespect, but I don't want to talk to or about your husband."

"Please, hear me out. This isn't about Curtis, and we didn't go through with the wedding."

Her revelation took me by surprise since she and Curtis were both selfish and did only what benefited them. I wondered why the wedding fell through.

"Okayyy, so, what's up? We can't discuss Quest either. You don't know me well, at all, actually. But you should know that I am team Quest, regardless, and I'm not getting between y'all beef, just like I expect you to stay out of Curtis's and my issues."

"Aubri, I don't want to put you in the middle of it. Just needed someone to hear me out. Quest won't. I don't see how he can expect me to fix anything when he won't give me the chance. I've done a lot of wrong in my life, but I love my son. I just want the chance to show him that much."

No one could understand how much I hated the fact that I was able to relate to Kourtney. We all made mistakes and knowing how badly I wanted Milani to forgive me for mine, I sympathized with her way more than I should have.

"Kourtney, I'll be honest with you. I understand. That's all I can say without overstepping my boundaries. I'll speak to Quest. I can't promise that he'll reach out to you, but I can promise you that I'll try."

"That's all I want. Thank you so much. You can give him this number, and I'll also text you my address."

After saying okay, I hung up. I didn't want to give her the chance to keep talking and dragging me into her pity party. In Quest's eyes, I probably said way more than I should have, but I could live with that. My attempt to get back to ironing after talking to Kourtney was futile. All I could think about was Milani. We hadn't spoken since the last time I saw her. She probably was going to ignore me, but I decided to shoot my shot.

Browsing through my phone, I headed to her contact information to send her a text message.

Hey, Milani. It's Aubri. I'm still respecting your decision to not be bothered with me. I just wanted to let you know that I was thinking about you. I'll probably never be able to make up for the lost time, but you should know that I'm willing to try. If ever you want to know me, I'm here. Teenage me didn't fully understand the decision I made and how it would affect the both of us, but now I see. You got the worse of it. I'm sorry. Honestly and truly sorry. If I would have felt just being who I am was good enough for you, believe me, I would have reached out a long time ago.

There was so much more that I wanted to say but I couldn't. I was a sobbing my mess, so I just sent what I had. When my phone started ringing, I could literally see a glimmer of hope twinkle around me, but it wasn't Milani, it was Quest.

"Hey, you." I did my best to mask the state I was in, but knowing Quest, he heard the sadness in my tone.

"What's wrong with you? You crying?"

Thought about lying, but decided to tell him the truth. Well, everything except the fact that I spoke to Kourtney; that was something I would have to ease on him at a later date.

"Baby, stop crying. Please. I told you everything between you and Milani would be alright. She needs time and so do you. When the time is right, things will fall into place for the both of you. You gotta work on forgiving yourself. Eventually, she'll forgive you too."

Maybe telling him about Kourtney's call did fit in this conversation.

"What about you?"

"Huh? What about me? I been told you I forgave you for not telling me about Milani. I'm off that. I'm looking forward to her coming around and shit being sweet."

"Thank you, but not that. Will you ever forgive Kourtney?"

It sounded like he punched something but I wasn't sure. "Why the fuck would you bring her up? Totally different situation. You nothing like that weak ass bitch," Quest snarled.

"Please, stop yelling. I didn't mean to get you upset, babe. I'm just trying… just forget it. I'm sorry." I was banking on my tone softening his and it worked.

"You don't have to apologize. Just don't compare situations. Kourt is scum. You're not."

My phone vibrated against my cheek, alerting me of a notification.

"Hold on, Quest."

Pulling the phone away from my ear, I looked at the screen and saw that it was a text from Milani.

Milani: I can't say that I can forgive you today or tomorrow, but I'm willing to try.

The message was simple but held so much weight. Of course, I had to share it with Quest.

"I told you, time is all y'all need. She has a lot to work through and process."

"You were right. You always are."

"Thank me when I come in the crib?"

Of course, he allowed his dirty little mind to creep into our conversation.

"Only if you hurry. I have an early morning tomorrow," I told him.

"On my way. I love you."

"I love you, too."

I ended the call with a smile on my face and feeling as if a weight had been lifted off my shoulders. Just as I was about to get back to getting my clothes together, another message came through. This time it was from Ashlynn.

Ashy: I spoke to Cross. I'll pick you up at eight. We'll grab coffee before heading to the office.

I laughed while texting her back.

A deal is a deal. See you in the morning.

Was definitely looking forward to seeing her the next day so she could share what happened with Cross with me, and I could share my news as well.

Lia

No one understood how much I hated getting up for the door. No matter how hard I wished people away when they rung the bell, it never worked. I didn't give up hope though. After two minutes of wishing away this visitor, I finally got up to answer it.

"Who is it?" I called out as I approached the door.

"Trey."

After unlocking the door, I held it open and stepped to the side so that he could come in. They really didn't waste anytime. It had only been a few days since I called Trey to let him know the plans my boyfriend had for him and set up their meet; now here he was on my doorstep.

"What took you so long to come to the door? That nigga ain't tell you I was coming?" He didn't even bother greeting me.

That's how little I meant to Quest's friends. I bet he greeted Aubri. Quest probably would shoot his ass if he didn't.

"Yeah, he told me. I'm like a million-months pregnant. Sorry I can't move at the speed of lightening."

"Heard you. You got that for me?"

Turning around, I grabbed the envelope off the side table and handed it to Trey.

"Why you doing this, Trey?"

He looked at me oddly.

"That's a funny question coming from you. You doing the same shit, Lia."

He was right in a sense. But Quest actually wronged me. I doubted highly he did anything to Trey. Almost certain he was doing this because the price was right.

"I'm sure it's different. Quest was good to you guys."

"And he was good to you," he retorted. "Quest was cool in my book until he wasn't. Nigga started icing me out and just turning to Quavo. How long you expect a nigga to play a side chick. I ain't sign up for that shit. I'm on the streets to get money. That's it. The other shit's for the birds."

All I could do was nod because I understood where Trey was coming from all too well.

"Plus, I got mouths to feed. Quest won't have control over how much I could do for me and mine because he chooses to give one nigga more money than the other. Type bitch shit is that."

"Yeah, I feel you. Quest don't even realize all the bridges he's burning."

"He don't. But I'm not the nigga that's gonna send him a boat. Let me get low though, Lia. You take care of yourself and that load."

"Yeah, you take care too, Trey."

After waiting for him to leave, I closed and locked the door behind him. All I could do was shake my head at all that was going on.

CHAPTER SEVEN

Quest

Parked across the street, I peered through my tinted window at Aubri. She was standing outside of the office laughing at whatever Ashlynn was saying. This is the element I liked seeing my girl in. Life wasn't perfect, but it was far from bad. She had a lot to smile about. I'd been peeping how she'd been working hard and shit, busting her ass to prove that she belonged at Ashlynn's company. She would complain to me at night about her feeling as if she didn't belong, because she didn't go to college, or work her way into the position she had. Even though being on the streets was nothing like working corporate, I explained to her that regardless of the credentials you start with, you grind 'til niggas respect the position you are earning. And that's what she'd been doing.

She and Ashy started toward Ashlynn's car. They were really on some carpool, let's meet up for breakfast and go home together after work, type shit. Not today, though. I wanted to surprise my baby girl.

"Ayo, shorty," I called out after emerging from my car. I turned, facing the side of the street they were on, and leaned against the car.

Aubri looked across the street and started cheesing like a kid in an amusement park.

"What's up, bro?" Ashlynn waved, before turning to hug Aubri.

"What's good, sis? You don't have to drop my baby home today."

Ashlynn shrugged. "Her lost. No Taco Tuesday for her at the spot."

Damn, I totally forgot it was Tuesday and they usually went to Patron Mexican Grill for tacos and drinks. Aubri didn't object, so I figured she didn't mind missing one Tuesday.

"Sorry."

Happily, Aubri skipped across the street. I met her on the passenger side of the car and pulled her into me.

"What a nice surprise," she whispered as she pulled her lips away from mine.

I opened the passenger side door, and leaned in to grab the Edible Arrangements.

"Somebody was thinking about you," I told her as I moved to the side so that she could get in the car.

Once she was seated, I handed her the fruit, closed the door, and walked over to the driver's side to join her.

"Ahh, I'm about to smash all this on the way home. Thank you, baby."

Looking over in her direction, I smirked. "As much as I want to take all the credit, I can't. I went to see my grandmoms and took her out. On our way back to her spot, we passed Edible Arrangements and she was like, 'remember when Aubri bought me some arrangements?' She wanted to go cop you something. She spent my bread but it was her idea."

"I love her, man. I know she is watching her stories right now and will just rush me off the phone, so I'll call and thank her later."

"I'm glad you know. She don't play about her stories."

As I slid into traffic, something on Aubri's phone caught her attention. Shorty was smiling and giggling like a schoolgirl.

"Damn, not even I make you laugh like that," I stated, faking as if I was jealous.

"It's Milani. She's telling me about some boy who thinks they go together because he bought her a soda."

"Ahh, we at that stage already?" I sighed.

"I know, right. Boys! I'm not ready," Aubri laughed. "She's not interested, though. Thank goodness."

"Not yet."

She typed another message before putting her phone in her bag and looking over at me.

"You know, we been texting more and more lately."

"That's good, Aubs. I'm happy y'all relationship is moving in the right direction. Y'all dead ass deserve to have each other. We gonna need her around soon enough."

Aubri cocked her head to the side and smirked. With one hand on the wheel, I reached over and rubbed her thigh, hiking her skirt up in the process.

"Who gonna baby sit when we have date night?" I asked, while sliding my hand a little higher until I felt the trim of her panties.

"Baby..." Her words were cut short when I pressed my pointer finger against her pearl.

"Yeah, baby. You gonna give me a seed, Aubs?" Slowly, I rotated my fingers on her clit, applying the right amount of pressure.

She swatted my hand away and blushed, flexing like she didn't want what she knew was coming. Unfortunately for her, her pussy betrayed her 'cause when I moved my hand, the proof was all over my fingers.

"Yeah, we can talk now, but you already know what it's hitting for when we get in the crib."

She laughed and turned toward the window so I wouldn't see the big ass smile on her face. Even after everything we've encountered thus far, she still pretended to be shy with me.

"Nah, forreal though. Tell me about your day, baby."

She turned toward me and lit up. She was dead ass excited to tell me about the shit she had been doing at work and the text exchanges with Milani, and I was all ears. It's the least I could do for her. She always listened to me and my stories without complaints, so I gave her that same respect. Plus, I wanted her to get it out now 'cause all I wanted to hear when we got in the house was skin slapping.

I already knew when we got in the crib, Aubri was going to try to be on her little teasing shit. Little did she know was that I had plans on fucking her wherever I caught her. If it was the foyer, on the steps that led upstairs, wherever, she was getting dicked down. She took her slow time letting us into the house, and when she finally did, she took off running toward the kitchen. That was cool with me. I followed her little ass, and when I caught her, threw her on top of the counter.

"Oh, I'm just light as a feather, huh?" She giggled while wiggling side to side.

I was standing between her legs with my hands planted on each side of her. She wasn't going nowhere.

"You really wanted me to chase you?" I spoke before leaning toward her and taking her bottom lip between my teeth.

"A little game of cat and mouse never hurt nobody," she purred.

My dick was bulging against my jeans, begging to be free. While releasing the hold I had on Aubri's lip, I slipped my hand up her skirt and slowly inched her panties down. Without coaching, she spread her legs wider, anticipating what was to come. Pulling myself away from her, I slowly got down on my knees in front of her and used my fingers to assault her love box. I've had my share of good pussy, but this pussy was the best. Her shit was tight as hell, and she got wetter than the Nile. With the remnants of juices leaking down my fingers, I licked them as I stood and undid my pants. Wrapping her legs around my waist, Aubri pulled me closed to her and leaned in for a kiss. Our tongues did a slow dance as she reached down and massaged my dick. With every stroke, my shit grew harder. Feeling my veins pulse in her palm had Aubri grinning. Without breaking our kiss, I moved my hands out the way, giving her space to do her thing. Her baby soft hands guided my piece inside her. Slowly, she filled herself with every inch of me.

After sliding her to the very edge of the counter, I tugged her shirt over her head and I pulled her off, leaving her ass resting in the palm of my hands. Aubri secured her hands around my neck and bounced up and down on my shit.

"Yeah, baby. Bounce on daddy's dick," I insisted.

Due to pleasure, her nipples stiffened and cut into me. They were taunting me, asking for attention. While still guiding her up and down my beef, I leaned my head down and assaulted each of her nipples with my tongue. Aubri wanted to be in control and for the first time, I allowed her. She worked herself on me effortlessly. The way she would grip my dick with her walls and release, mixed with the way her juices dripped down my leg, was too much. She was having her fun and it was time to have mine. Raising her up enough for my dick to slide out of her, I placed her down on her feet. She looked up at me with sadness in her eyes.

"I was enjoying that."

"You'll enjoy this more."

Quickly, I spun her around and she propped her elbows up on the counter. Reaching forward, I palmed both her titties and used them as handles to drive myself into her from the back.

Aubri gasped and tossed her head back into my chest.

"Fuck, Quest," she cried out.

Bending my knees a little, I pushed in deeper. She gripped the edge of the granite counter as hard as she could as she tossed her ass back at me and I met each thrust.

"You gonna have my seed, Aubri?" I moaned while slapping her ass and grinding into her.

"Yesssss," she cried out.

My plan was to shoot her shit up regardless, but having her verbal permission made it even more satisfying. With each stroke, I could feel my nut building up. Aubri's body shook violently beneath me as she cried out for me to go deeper and not to stop. She didn't have to worry about that because I had no intentions on stopping. At least not until I went over the edge she just went over, as her body rocked from the orgasm she was experiencing.

"Fuck," I grunted as my knees wobbled, threatening to give out on me.

Shorty had my shit shaking as much as she was shaking.

"Damn, Aubri." Leaning over, I moaned into her hair, releasing a stream of my semen in her guts.

Her body fell limp over the counter as I pulled out.

"I love you, Quest." She didn't even have the energy to face me.

My energy was depleted as well, but we still had to make it upstairs.

"I love you, too." I swept her up in my arms and carried her up to the room. After placing her down on the bed, I sat on the edge and zoned out. It wasn't on purpose. It was just that no matter how good the pussy was, and trust me, it was good, other shit I had going on still found its way to my thoughts, and she sensed that.

"What's wrong?" She pulled herself up and rested her head against my back.

"Julio called me earlier. Cross and I gotta go on the road for a few days. Just thinking about all that's been going on and shit, we really haven't had a moment to just sit back and enjoy being us. When I first met you, we did shit. Nothing major, but we kicked it. Little date nights and shit. It's just different now. You haven't even been leaving me chocolate kisses around the house."

"It has been a little hectic lately. It's so much that we're both trying to transition into. We'll find a balance and we'll get back to being us. Don't worry, baby. I'll send you on your trip with some kisses." She placed a gentle kiss on the back of my shoulder. "I love you, and thank you for being here for me. I know you have a lot going on with your work, so I'm not stressing it. I know that when I need you, you'll be here, no questions asked."

"Of course I will. I love you too. I promise, once Cross and I get into the routine of how shit runs with our new positions, things will be different. Better."

"You don't need to promise me that. Just promise that you'll make it home in one piece."

"Definitely, Aubs. I can't leave you, yet."

She twisted up her lips and shook her head.

"No time soon."

Turning a little toward her, I pushed her back on the bed, going down with her, and buried my face in the crook of her neck. After nibbling on her neck a minute, I lifted myself up a little, stared at her, and sincerely told her, "Not if I can help it."

CHAPTER EIGHT

Quest

After a week on the road in Miami, all I wanted to do was slide up in Aubri's pussy and pass the fuck out after. A nigga was dead tired, but not too tired to pass up on smashing my shorty after not getting none for a week. Cross's whip came to a complete stop in front of my crib, causing me to sigh in relief.

"Nigga, what are you sighing for? You had me drive the whole ten hours. And you tired? The fucking nerve!"

Couldn't even find the energy to laugh at his dumb ass. Just smirked and closed my eyes for a second.

"You home; go up and go to bed," Cross insisted.

"Yeah. But yo, we really making this shit happen." 'Til this day, I was still in shock at how we managed to handle the amount of work Julio entrusted us with. Our hours were longer and we spent a lot more time away from home than we liked to, but shit was worth it. I mean, home was taken care of and my bank account was consistently increasing. Wasn't much to complain about. Niggas went to Miami to secure distributors that Julio didn't think we could secure, and we did.

"We are. Not even going to hold you. I thought you and the nigga, Julio, was crazy talking, that five hundred bricks a shipment shit, but look at the level up."

"Yeah, shit is good right now. A little too good," I admitted.

Cross turned toward me. "What you mean by that, bro?" he questioned.

I thought about getting deeper into this feeling I was having, but decided against. I needed Cross's head to be one hundred percent in the game and clear of doubt. The feelings that I was having about shit going left could completely fuck up his thought process, and neither one of us could afford that.

"Nothing. Hit me when you get home," I instructed him.

For a minute, I had this feeling that shit was about to get bad for us, and I couldn't shake it no matter how hard I tried. It wasn't a scared bone in my body, so of course I planned for it to be business as usual until some shit came up that we had to handle, but the constant thoughts I was having were nagging the fuck out of me. If something was going to happen, I wanted it hurry up and happen so we could deal with it and move forward, just like we've done every other issue from the past.

"Yeah, iight. I will. Tell Aub's I said what's good."

"Will do."

Before pushing open the door, I gave Cross dap and got out. Making my way up the driveway with my head buried in my phone,

I browsed through emails. One was from a realtor I had been kicking it with back and forth on some property. It was the exact email I was waiting on. I hadn't spoken to Aubri about the potential move, but I knew that she'd understand. With how shit was moving now with Julio, living on a regular ass block wasn't going to cut it. I mean, my spot was secure, but at the same time, better precautions would be to have me and my shorty laying our head somewhere tucked away and low-key. Gave Cross the same advice, but I didn't expect him to listen. When it came to shit outside of business, he did what he wanted on his own time.

After using my key to let myself in, I walked in on laughter coming from the living room. Ash's car wasn't out front, so I didn't know who the other female's voice belonged to. Didn't take me long to find out though. Posted up against the frame of the entrance to the living room, I looked on as Aubri and Milani shared a genuine laugh. The shit warmed my heart. I knew they had been keeping in touch via text and phone calls here and there, but seeing them here together was huge, and I was happy it was finally happening.

"Babe! I didn't even hear you come in," Aubri squealed while pouncing to her feet and jogging over to me.

Pulling her into me, I rested my head in the crook of her neck and inhaled.

"I missed the shit out of you," I whispered. "Milani, what's good? Very nice to see you." I shifted my eyes above Aubri's shoulder and connected with Milani's.

She smiled a warm smile before waving. "Hey, Quest. It's good to see you as well. You have a very nice home."

"Thank you." Aubri was still pressed against me with her arms wrapped around me. I had to slide back and pull her away from me. Although that's not what I really wanted to do, Milani was present. I was longing for her pussy, but their reunion was long overdue. I wasn't coming in between that.

"Y'all good?" I looked from Milani then down at Aubri.

She nodded and placed her hand on my chest.

"We're good. How was your trip? Everything, everything?"

Aubri had this new shit where she wanted to be filled in about my day to day. Of course, I was a little hesitant because I felt the less she knew, the better; but at the same time; it felt good having someone to share shit with who wasn't a part of it. She just offered a listening ear and sometimes, an opinion when I asked for one. However, Milani was here so I wasn't going to get into that.

"It was cool. I'ma leave you ladies to it, though. I'm tired as hell." After kissing Aubri, I took a few steps away from her.

"Quest, wait," she called after me.

Turning on my heels, I waited for her to speak her peace.

"I'll be right back, Milani." She walked over toward me and ushered me toward the kitchen. "So…" she started.

Whenever she started a sentence with 'so' or 'well,' I knew she was about to say some shit I didn't want to hear or wouldn't like.

"What happened, Aubs?"

She looked away and sighed. "Curtis reached out to me again. Of

120

course I didn't answer because I really don't have anything to say still."

If she didn't answer, what was the need for her to tell me he called again. I was wondering who was gonna reach out first between him and Kourtney. Wondered if they went through with the wedding. Didn't really give a fuck, because nothing would change between me and Aubri, but I still wondered.

"I know you probably going to spazz out, but I spoke to Kourtney. Twice, actually."

My body tensed up, hearing her name. What the fuck did she have to say to Aubri?

"She said she's still been trying to reach you, but she didn't have a working number for you, and your grandmother wouldn't give her the number unless you told her she could. Of course, I wasn't giving her your number, but I do think you should take her information and reach out, Quest."

"Did they get married?"

She shrugged. "Don't know, but she said he didn't live there. As soon as she mentioned him, I cut her off."

"Oh, iight. I'm going to shower and sleep."

"Quest."

I walked around her toward the stairs, but stopped suddenly and turned to find her leaning against the wall by the kitchen, gawking at me as if she knew I was going to turn around.

"Text me the address."

Instead of heading upstairs, I headed back out the door. If

Kourtney took it upon herself to reach out, I was going to hear her out. This was the first time she ever did that. Had to see what changed. Aubri joined me at the front door but didn't attempt to stop me. Instead, she hugged me and told me to be safe.

"Texting you now," she called out as I made my way over to my car.

<>

When I pulled up to the address Aubri texted me, I sat outside contemplating my next move. What the fuck would I say to the woman I spent my entire life hating? Why would I even show up at her spot? I don't know if it was seeing Aubri with Milani that made feel like this was the right decision or not. I just know that shit never went well with Kourtney. She was nowhere near an easy person to deal with, but I was already here. So fuck it.

Climbing out of the car, I slammed the door closed behind me and hit the lock button on the key fob as I made my way toward the front door. I looked around cautiously taking in my surroundings before ringing the bell.

"Qu—Quest," she stuttered as she opened the door. "Come in."

She stepped aside before I could say anything. Walking in, I looked around the spot. From what I could see, the spot had a nice layout but it was type empty.

"Just moved in?" I questioned, once I spotted the boxes stacked in the corner.

"Yeah. Was supposed to be our place after the wedding, but before I get into that, I'm glad you came. You're a hard man to track down."

"I've heard. What's up, though? Why you reached out, Kourtney?"

"Come on in the living room. I have some folding chairs."

She led the way toward the living room, and I slowly followed her trail. After taking a seat on one of the hard ass steel chairs, I looked to her for an explanation.

"I'm sorry," she whispered.

"What?" was the only thing that I could say because I couldn't believe that she was apologizing for something. Kourtney was always right. Even when she knew she was wrong, she still believed and tried to convince you that she was right.

"I've been horrible to you, Quest. You think I don't know that or regret it, but I do. By the time I'd really come to, with all the wrong I'd done when it came to you, you were living and doing your thing. How could I step in and disrupt your life because I woke up one morning and decided I wanted to be your mother?"

"The way you're attempting to do it now," I stated flatly.

How you say you didn't want to disrupt my life but then turn around and do just that? To be honest, her apology came too many years too late. I was already the man I was going to be. When I needed my mother, she needed the streets and random ass niggas, so this come to Jesus moment she was trying to have was a dub.

"I know what you're thinking. I'm not even trying to jump in the role of Mom right now, Quest. One day, I hope that you'll see me as your mom and allow me to be in your life that way, but right now, I just want peace. I want us to be able to speak, share a meal, baby steps."

"I'm glad you know that you'll never be able to step in as Mom. When I needed you, Kourtney, you said fuck me. Not those exact words, but your actions, man. You see me out here doing my thing, living my life, but you missed out on my struggles. You missed the nights I cried myself to sleep because my mother didn't love me. You missed all the times my grandmother had to find excuses for you because you flaked. Every graduation, every birthday, Christmas... wait, one Christmas you sent me a Hess truck." I paused to take a breath and laugh at the fact that out of all my Christmases, all I got from the woman that brought me into the world was a fucking Hess truck. "I'm your fucking son! Who just decides that they don't want to be a mother when they have the means to? Nothing was wrong with you. You had money, you had support, no addiction issues, you dead ass just decided that you weren't going to be a mother."

"Quest," she attempted to butt in.

"Nah, let me talk my shit. As if abandoning me wasn't enough, you popped up with another kid who you seemed to love the life out of. Even as a grown ass man, that shit affected me. What did Mason offer you that I didn't? How was loving one son and not the other easy for you? You're a fucked-up individual, Kourtney, but I dead ass forgive you. Not because you deserve my forgiveness, but because I'm tired of walking around with this shit on my chest. Hating you takes too much energy, man. It's time for me to let it go."

My chest heaved up and down, even moments after I stopped giving her my spiel. All that shit I had been holding in needed to be said.

"Yo, Kourtney."

I froze hearing that voice before slowly looking up toward the entrance of the living room. When my eyes landed on him, I sprang from my seat.

"What the fuck is he doing here? I thought you told Aub he didn't live here?" I barked.

"Fuck you mean? I paid for this house, nigga. You not going to come in—"

Lunging at him, I threw a hook that connected with his jaw. He stumbled backward before falling to the floor and shuffling away from me. I wasn't done though.

"What were you about to say, nigga? Talk that hot shit now," I roared while throwing another jab in his direction.

"Stop it! Quest, get off him," Kourtney wailed in the background.

Her screams took me off my square allowing Curtis to get a hit in. I bounced back by landing two to his midsection.

"Quest," The tiny whisper was enough to bring me back from the dark place I found myself in. Slowly, I looked up at the top of the steps and found Mason standing there looking down at me hovering over Curtis, who I was assuming was his dad. Pulling myself up, I took a few steps back.

"Mase, what's up, bro? We were just wrestling," I lied.

"Mason, go back to your room, and don't come out until I come get you," Kourtney instructed him.

He looked at me for another second before retreating to his room.

"Un-fucking-believable. You in here apologizing to me but you still with this nigga? He's my shorty's brother. Still picking niggas over your family. You ain't sorry. Well actually, yeah, you are."

Curtis was still sitting on the floor, holding his jaw. I stepped over the nigga to make my way to the front door.

"He's leaving. He's here getting him and Mason's things. I meant everything I said to you, Quest. Do I love Curtis? Yes. But I know that I couldn't keep this going and try to fix my relationship with you, so for once, I'm picking you. I'm putting you first."

"What you mean he came for him and Mason things? You letting this nigga take ya son? You want to walk that path again?"

"It's not even like that, Quest. Mason isn't my son. Well, not biologically. When I met Curtis, he already had Mason, I just took him in and loved him like that son I didn't have."

"Didn't have? Like the son you tossed to the side, you mean."

She sighed and rubbed the side of her temples. This was too much. I didn't come here for this shit and was over listening to it.

"What you want from me? A hug? A kiss on the forehead. You grown now, Quest. Let's handle this like two grown people. The 'my mommy didn't love me shit' is played out for you as a grown ass man, okay."

"Yeah, you right. You're a dub. This whole situation is a dub," I told her.

"You going through all this trouble for my sister. You have no idea how used and washed up that bitch is, dude."

I dove back over in Curtis's direction and grabbed his throat. "What the fuck you said?" I hissed through gritted teeth.

Without releasing the hold I had on his neck, I reached into the waist of my jeans and pulled out my silenced nine. Shoving the barrel against his temple, I repeated the question I previously asked him.

"Quest, please. Put that away. Mason is right upstairs, you do not want to do this."

Curtis's eyes were bulging out of his head as the oxygen level in his body quickly depleted. I wasn't letting him go though. If the nigga died right there on the floor of their crib, it didn't matter to me. The only thing that caused me to loosen the grip I had on his throat was the thought of how affected Aubri would be if I did kill him.

"If you ever say her name again, I'll kill you, my nigga. That's a fucking promise. Stay the fuck away from her, don't call, none of that."

I eased the gun away from his temple and stood up. Even after almost having the life squeezed out of his body, he still decided to talk shit.

"She really got you fooled. You never questioned why she didn't have nobody. Why nobody fucking wanted her? You think your mother so fucked up, Aubri ain't no better. You must didn't meet Milani yet."

Hearing him mention Milani's name caused me to aim my pistol at his shoulder and pulled the trigger.

Pop!

'Cause it meant one thing.

"You knew?"

"Fuck," he wailed before reaching over with his left hand and pressing it against his right shoulder. As expected, Kourtney was at his side hyperventilating like I shot the nigga in a vital organ. I should have.

"You knew?" I repeated with my gun still aimed at him.

"Knew what? That she fucked my best friend then claimed he raped her."

I knew the facts, thanks to Stephanie admitting it and because Aubri shared the fucking details. I could have shot him again for being scum, but I wasn't going to. He was gonna feel pain though. Leaning over him, I smacked Kourtney's hand away, found his wound and dug my finger into the tiny hole.

He squirmed and screamed but I didn't let up.

"You feel that. That pain that's coursing through your body. Imagine what your sister felt when your scum ass friend was forcing himself on her. You could tell yourself that she made it up or whatever, if that's what helps you sleep at night. But again, Curtis, come near her, say her name, breathe in her direction, and I will blow your fucking brains out. Kourtney, you sorry, right? You know what to do then."

Pulling my finger out of the hole in his shoulder, I wiped the blood off with his shirt and dipped. Curtis was a street nigga. I wasn't worried about him running to twelve. If he wanted to do something about what I did to him, he would see me in the street. If I was lucky, Kourtney and Mason would be nowhere around and I'd get to finish the nigga off.

"Call Aubri," I instructed my car as I drove off.

I thought about how I would tell her what went down at Kourt's crib but decided against it. She ain't want shit to do with the nigga Curtis anyway. If it came up later, we'd discuss it; if not, whatever.

Aubri

"Hold on, Milani. Let me see what Quest wants." We were in the middle of making lunch when my phone started ringing. After wiping my hands on the towel, I grabbed my phone off the counter and slid my finger across the screen to answer.

"What's up, bae?"

"You good?" Quest questioned.

"Umm, yeah. I'm home still with Milani, making lunch. Where are you? Are you okay?"

"Yeah. I love you, Aubri."

"I love you too. You sure you good?'"

"Yeah. I'll be back home in a minute. I'm on my way now."

Before I could respond, he hung up. The brief exchange was weird to me, so before going back to cooking with Milani, I shot him a text.

Phone call was a little strange. You sure you okay? Don't lie to me, Quest.

I set the phone back on the counter and rested against it, expecting a text to come through from him right away. But after a minute and no reply, I turned back to Milani who was checking on the garlic bread.

"That food smells so good, my stomach is growling."

"Mine too. I'm surprised you didn't hear it." Milani laughed while rubbing her stomach in a circular motion.

Words would never be able to describe how thankful I was for this moment. However, I still didn't understand how we got to this point. My bell rung one day, and it was Milani and Stephanie. Stephanie asked if it was okay if she hung out for a few hours because she wanted to see me, and of course, I said yes. But that was it. Milani came in making jokes, acting as if she just didn't want anything to do with me. I didn't want to upset her or bring up old wounds, but I thought it was necessary for us to move forward.

"Thank you, for wanting to see me. You have no idea how much this has made my day. My year, actually."

"You want to know what made me change my mind?"

"Honestly, yes."

She climbed up on the stool to the counter and made herself comfortable.

"Today, I woke up and my mom did something. I was like yo, I'd never do something like that. It sounds weird or whatever, but it just made me think about who I got certain parts of myself from. Like, if you'd do something one day and I'd ever be able to say, 'oh, I do that too.' Or 'now I see where I get that from.' It just made me realize how much I really do want to get to know you. At the end of the day, you're my mom. I love my mother. I mean, she's the absolute best, but I can't pretend that you don't exist. It won't ever change the fact that I'm adopted. I figured the worse that could happen is wouldn't have a relationship, but I still would have my mother, and the best thing that could happen is our relationship will blossom and I'll have twice the love."

For thirteen, she was well spoken. No, she didn't use big fancy words, but she knew how to properly communicate how she was feeling. Not to mention, everything she said completely resonated with me. I understood and appreciated every bit of it.

"I'd love for you to get to know me and vice versa. Anytime you want to spend time with me, I'll be here. Never in your life will I abandon you again. If you push me away, I'll still be here if you decide to come back. Forever. I promise, Milani."

"Aubri… It is okay if I call you Aubri, right?"

I nodded.

"I don't want you to think that I don't feel for you and what you experienced when you were younger. I'm not selfish or oblivious to the fact that you went through something traumatizing. I don't think I was abandoned by you at all. I actually wanted to thank you. I've heard horror stories, from people in school, the news, social media, everywhere, and I know that things could have turned out horrible for me, and it didn't, because you were selfless enough to know you couldn't care for me. It just sucks, going your whole life not knowing that there's this whole other world you are connected to that you know nothing about."

"Can I hug you?"

Tears were on the brink of escaping. I couldn't find the words to express what I was feeling after what she said, so a hug had to suffice. She opened her arms wide and I stepped forward, wrapping mine around her.

"Thank you for giving me a chance."

I inhaled the aroma that floated around the kitchen before checking my watch and deciding it was time to take the food out. After making a plate for Milani and myself, I joined her at the counter and we dug in.

To my surprise, conversation flowed freely. The pressure of me being her mother and her being my child was nonexistent. We were just two people chatting and getting to know each other.

"So, you really vegan, huh? I don't think I could live without my chicken. Oh my God."

Laughing, I picked up our plates and carried them over to the sink to wash.

"Chicken was the hardest for me to give up. But, I'm fake vegan. I eat seafood, so they called that a pescatarian, although my new year's resolution is to give up seafood as well."

She shook her head wildly. "So, I should expect to eat grass whenever I visit."

We both burst out laughing.

"No, Quest is farrrr from vegan. Whenever you're here, we'll have seafood or I'll make whatever for you and Quest and have a little bowl of grass for myself."

"Oh, good. Aubri, do I have grandparents from you?"

Struggling to mask my true feelings about her question, I put on a fake smile. Inside I was dying. The reminder that my parents were no longer here to help me navigate life, was something I still struggled with all these years later.

"My parents died."

"I'm sorry. I do remember now, when you were telling me what happened you mentioned that. I'm sorry for bringing it up."

I placed my hand on her shoulder. "No need to apologize. I do have a grandmother, who I'd love for you to meet one day. She stays in a care facility upstate."

"That'll be cool. I'll get to see how I'ma look when I'm up there in age."

"Yeah, kid. You definitely got that sense of humor from me."

Switching gears a bit, I directed some questions at her. I didn't want her to feel as if she was on an interview, so I just brought up random topics just to get her views on them, and learned a lot about her in the process.

"Milani, what do you want from me moving forward?" She probably wasn't expecting that question, but I needed to know. I didn't want to place any pressure on her or move in a way that would drive her back out of my life.

"Umm, honestly. Just consistency. And patience. Lots of patience. I'm still wrapping my head around this, so bear with me. But that's all I ask. Be here when you say you will, keep your word, be honest, and just accept me. I'm a 'you get what you see' type of girl."

"As am I, so I can definitely respect that. And I will be consistent and have patience."

Milani was about to speak, but paused when her phone vibrated. After tending to whatever, she looked up at me.

"That was my mom. She's five minutes away."

Again, I had to hide how I felt about my time being cut so short, and remind myself to be patient.

"Okay, no problem."

"But, I already told her. This is not how I want it. You know, coming with you for like an hour or two at a time randomly. We had this long conversation about what I wanted and stuff, and I told her. Eventually, I want to spend weekends with you, and maybe rotate holidays or even spend some time with you and my mom together. I'm open to having that type of relationship, if you are."

"Of course I am. We'll let it all flow naturally, and whatever you and your mother are comfortable with, so am I. I've never had sleepovers and stuff like that, so that'll be fun. Girl talk, and mani/pedis." I laughed before leaning in and hugging her.

As if on cue, the bell rung and I already knew it was Stephanie.

"Welp, let's not leave her waiting."

Milani slid off the stool, gave me another hug, and made her way to the front door.

"Thank you for letting me hang out."

"You're welcome over here any time, Milani."

Slowly, I opened the door, dreading that our time was coming to an end, and there was Stephanie bright eyed and bushy tailed.

After greeting Stephanie, Milani told her that she'd wait in the car. I guess she just assumed that we would want to talk in private and we did. Well, at least I did.

"I hope we didn't ambush you," Stephanie started.

I shook my head no. "Not at all. Thank you for this. We needed it."

"She knows what she wants, Aubri. I can't tell the girl no as long as it's within thirteen-year-old limits, and you were never meant to be off limits. You know that, right?"

"I do."

"She mentioned eventually wanting to stay over a few nights and all this stuff. She's really excited to have you a part of her life. Even if she doesn't show it. She just doesn't want to be let down or hurt, you know."

"I know. And you know I'd never hurt her."

"Of course I know that. Which is why I have no objections. We are family, whichever way you choose to look at it. Just as you trusted me with her, I trust you with our girl. I won't come between whatever is meant to happen here, as long as we stay on the same page."

"Definitely. Thank you, again."

"No, thank you. And don't worry, next time I'll make her call first."

We laughed, hugged, and just like that, she and Milani were gone, leaving me alone with my thoughts.

CHAPTER NINE

Quest

Sleep is something I'd been lacking since I got back in town. Stepping up in Julio's organization was becoming more time consuming than I thought. For once, I found myself enjoying a deep sleep without the worry of having to get up bright and early and dip out. Clearly, niggas had other plans for me because my phone wanted to ring off the hook. Even with the shit on vibrate, all I heard was it rattling on the nightstand. For a while, I didn't bother picking it up to see who it was because that's how badly I needed and wanted that sleep. However, after five times, I knew I had to answer. Not to mention, Aubri was damn near climbing over me to get it.

"Aight, I'm gonna get it, get off me," I mumbled beneath her.

Her body was stretched across mine and her elbow was damn near taking my eye out.

"Nope. You should have answered the first seventeen, thirty-eight times it rang." By this time, she was rolling off of me with the phone in her hand.

"Hello… Yep, he's right here. Hold on." She reached her arm back over to me with the phone in her palm. "It's Cross."

Immediately, I knew that I fucked up and should have answered on the first ring. After taking the phone from Aubri, I pressed it against my ear and pulled myself up in the bed.

"Yo."

"My nigga, what's good with you? Nigga, Quavo been blowing your phone up then started blowing my shit up," Cross vented. "These niggas got us."

"What? What niggas?" By this time, I was getting out of the bed. I knew that no matter what he said next, I would be leaving the crib, so I got a head start.

"Both trucks were stopped by DEA." He paused. I don't know if it was for effect or what, but the fucking silence on top of the realization of what he said was killing me.

"Nah, you not on my phone telling me no shit like that!" I roared. "How the fuck did that happen? Yo, meet me—"

"I'm like a block away from ya crib. Was going to wake your ass up one way or the other."

"Aight, I see you when you get here."

Without waiting for him to respond, I hung up and grabbed the shorts from the foot of the bed.

"Are you okay?"

I glanced back to find Aubri sitting up in the bed with the sheet pulled up, covering her naked body.

"Not really. But go back to sleep. Cross on his way over here. I won't leave without letting you know, aight?"

She leaned forward, dropping the sheet and exposing her perky titties. She ran her hand up and down my back, and surprisingly, that soothed me in a way that only her touch could.

"I love you, Quest."

"I love you too," I told her while slipping on my shorts.

After turning around and kissing her forehead, I got up and left out the room. The walk downstairs was long and dreading. For the life of me, I couldn't understand how a plan that was so fucking solid, went so wrong. A million things could have gone wrong. Things that I even expected when it came to moving product, but getting seized by the DEA wasn't on the list of those things. Knowing Cross, he would ring the bell even though it was almost four in the morning, and I didn't want him to wake Aubri back up, even though I was almost sure that she wasn't going to go back to sleep until I returned to bed. Opening the door, I stepped outside, not caring how exposed I was to the cool air.

I was burning the fuck up on the inside, so the weather wasn't fazing me. Seeing Cross's lights approaching, reminded me how exposed I was living in this spot. Making a move had to move up on my to-do list. Ashlynn had already sent me paperwork on a few spots, and Aubri was with whatever I decided; it was just time to make it happen, especially after this seize. I wasn't no dumb nigga. I knew this shit wasn't an accident. My route wasn't hot, I made sure of that.

"How this happened, son?" I asked Cross again as he walked up on me.

We gave each other a weak ass dap before walking into the crib.

"Can't even answer that, bro. You know we can't talk to the drivers. Quavo sending one of the stand by attorneys to them, so hopefully we'll have more information later on. All we got was a call from one of the drivers once he realized he was being tailed."

"This shit can't be happening right now. You know how this shit sets us back?" I stressed.

Five million dollars of product just fucking gone.

"We needed that shipment. When I say product is low, shit is low."

"You think I don't know that?"

That was the downside of getting the work off as fast as we were. Shipments were scheduled and rarely did we stray from that schedule. By the time it was time to re-up, we had already run through the previous shipment. With this load being seized, we were literally dry. No work at all. With three days to make something shake, because that's when our clients expected their work, I didn't know what the fuck we were going to do.

"You predicted this."

Figured he was referring to when I told him shit was a little too good. There was always some expectation of things going wrong because it just came with the territory. But I didn't predict this. This would have been the last thing I guessed that would happen to us.

"Quest, what's the plan?"

With my legs crossed on the coffee table, I was laying back on the couch with my eyes closed. This is when I hated being the nigga who always had the answers, because I really didn't have any right now.

"Before anything, we gotta get up with Julio." That was the only thing I knew. "I'm not even trying to link with this nigga without that five million."

Feeling the cushion on the couch sink a little told me that Cross had finally sat down. I was tired of him pacing but didn't bother saying anything.

"We could always have him front us two shipments."

"That's not going to work, Cross. This ain't no measly ass five hundred bands. Five M's. Nobody is taking that loss and trusting us with more product without the bread upfront. This is the wrong time for this shit to happen."

All the years we been in business, and we've never taken a hit like this. We had spots raided. Lost a few bricks, had money stolen, a few corner boys locked up, but nothing on this scale.

Finally opening my eyes, I looked over at Cross. "We can't go to him without the bread. I'ma set up a meet with him, but at the same time, I want to tell him we lost the product but here's the money. If we do shit the right way, he'll be more inclined to put a rush on the next shipment. Hopefully, we'll have it in time to supply these other niggas in three days."

Stress was written on Cross's face. He had to be having the same thoughts that I was.

"Bro, how we going to get five million and put together a new

141

delivery route for a shipment that Julio might or might not give us. And in the event that he doesn't want to give us all that product, who we going to fuck with?"

Not getting product from Julio wasn't an option. But Cross was right to wonder how we were going to pull shit off in three days.

"Y'all want me to make something to eat?"

Hearing her voice made me open my eyes and look toward the entrance of the living room. Aubri was standing there leaning against the wall, waiting for a response.

"I told you to go back to sleep, bae. We good."

She shook her head. "I'm going to the office at seven; figured I'd make sure you were straight first. What's up, Cross?"

Cross lifted his head from his lap and looked up at Aubri.

"My bad, sis. My head somewhere else. But I'm good too; thanks, though."

"It's not even five, Aubri. You can rest for like another hour." I hated that she got into the habit of only sleeping when I slept because that meant she barely rested.

"I'm okay. I'm going to shower."

After watching her disappear, I leaned back onto the couch, closing my eyes, and allowing my thoughts to roam. Next thing I knew, I was waking up due to the sun beaming through the living room window, tap dancing on my face. I looked over at Cross and he was leaning on the arm of the couch knocked out. I was happy for that; it gave me time to get my thoughts together without his questions.

Lia

*J*olting out of my sleep, I tossed my hand across my chest as if doing that would regulate my speeding heart rate. Using my free hand, I rubbed my eyes in an attempt to get them to adjust to the light that was shining through my bedroom window. The ringing of the bell didn't cease, so clearly, whoever it was that needed me, had no plans on leaving. It wasn't rocket science; I knew exactly who it was. I mean, besides the fact that I don't have any friends and none of my family would just pop up on me, it was the crack of dawn.

"I'm coming," I called out even though more than likely I wasn't heard.

After tossing my blanket back, I glanced down at my belly and watched for a minute as my daughter abused my insides. If I was being honest, I was completely over this pregnancy. Was at the point where I would cut myself open and deliver via a home C-section if I knew I would survive it. This shit was too much. Finally, I gained the energy to get out the bed and wobbled to the front door. As I reached for the knob, I was hit with a sharp pain that damn near crippled me, causing me to pause and lean against the wall until the pain subsided. Once stable, I leaned forward and peeked through the window to see who it was before opening the door.

"You did good," was the first thing he said before brushing past me and walking into the house.

"Umm, thanks, I guess."

"I want to see them dig themselves out of this hole." He laughed cynically. "What's wrong with you?" he noticed the disgruntled look on my face and questioned.

"A little pain. That's all."

"Oh."

Oh? All he offered me was oh? I followed behind him as he made his way to the kitchen.

"Why didn't you use your key?"

It took a real dick head to wake up a pregnant lady at seven in the morning when he could have easily used his key to let himself in.

"You need the exercise. I'm not trying to have you fat as shit after you have that baby. The walk from the bed to the door, ain't going to kill you."

Sucking my teeth, I slid onto the stool that was at the counter. I swear if he didn't put a roof over my head and keep my phone on, I would have been ghost. This relationship, if that's what I could even call it, started off great. I was fresh out of my mess with Quest and he provided the friend that I so desperately needed. It's true when they say a shoulder to cry on becomes a dick to ride on, because that's exactly how it happened. One minute, I was boo hoo'in to him about my problems. Not being able to pay for school, not having a stable place to sleep, and the list went on. Next thing I know, I was moving into this house he was renting for me, and he had me on my back whenever he pleased. As if that wasn't enough, the favors started kicking in. Every single one of them had something to do with Quest and Cross. I wondered what this latest favor costed them.

"What's going to happen to Quest?"

He never gave me the details. Just told me what to do and when to do it. Usually, I didn't ask questions, but now I was questioning everything, even myself.

"Does it matter?" he snapped.

Shrugging, I rested my elbows on the counter and leaned forward, resting my head in my hands.

"Sort of. He is the father of my child. I thought we had an understanding on that fact."

My boyfriend had no idea about the possibility of Cross or Sean being my daughter's dad, and if it was up to me, it would stay that way. At least until I was able to get away and provide for myself.

"And I thought we had an understanding that I didn't give a fuck. That nigga not here. He's your daughter's father but he didn't give a fuck to make sure that you had somewhere to lay your head. Does he go to your appointments and shit? Miss me with the act, like you care what happens to Quest. If you're wondering, he's not dead yet."

'Yet' haunted me. The plan was never to kill Quest. I'd never willingly participate in something that would eventually lead to his demise. Messing with his business was one thing, but I didn't wish death on him. I didn't want or need that karma.

"Having their shipment intercepted was the first step in a very well thought out plan. He ain't going to be able to recover from that loss. I'm sure it crippled him."

I had so many questions that I knew he wouldn't answer, so I decided to remain quiet and let him ramble. He would say enough for me to be able to piece together what went down and what would go down in the future. So far, I was getting my phone call to the police had probably got one of Quest's spots raided. That wasn't too bad because I knew Quest. He always had for a rainy day. If this nigga thought that a little raid would take him out, he didn't have such a well thought out plan as he thought.

He continued talking while looking through the refrigerator.

"He lost product and I know he don't have the money to cover it. Once his connect get wind of that, he'll be gunning for him. It's just a matter of time before his whole operation is over, and if I'm lucky, his life too."

"That wasn't part of the plan."

He turned around so fast and before I could react, he rushed over to me, grabbing me by the throat. One minute my ass was on the stool, and the next I was being held up against the wall by my throat.

"Me taking care of the next nigga's baby wasn't part of the plan either. Fuck you think this is?"

Gasping was all I could do. Words would take oxygen that I was losing at rapid speed. All I could think about was my baby. Just when I thought it couldn't get any worse, he moved me from against the wall and slammed me against it.

"You knew what it was from the beginning. Don't start playing dumb. As easy as I been making your life, I could make it worse. Don't test me."

Fear slithered through my body, incited by the malicious tone he used. I'd never seen this side of him used on me before, and it frightened me. Not so much for myself, but for the baby that was due to come into this world in a few weeks. What did I get myself into?

"I'm out. Was going to spend some time with you, but you found a way to ruin it. Wait for my call with the next set of instructions."

He loosened the hold he had on my throat and because I was too busy trying to catch my breath, I didn't respond to what he said. That pissed him off even more. He pounded his hand against the wall beside my head, causing me to jump.

"You heard what the fuck I said?"

Nervously, I nodded while silently dying inside.

"And the next time you speak to that nigga, Quest, be sure to let him know how you heard Trey snaked him."

I stood there frozen as he backed away from me and left. It wasn't until I heard the front door close, did I release the breath I was holding in and stepped away from the wall. Afraid that he would come back, I took my slow time to the door to lock it.

With my back against the door, I slowly slid to the floor. In life, I took so much for granted, and I was being paid back for that in the worst way. I wanted and needed to be different. I needed to go back to the girl I was pre-Quest. I won't blame him for the way my life was spiraling because as an adult with free will, I made the decisions I made. No one made them for me. Unfortunately, it was just turning out to be one bad decision after the other. The one I was currently making was panning out to be the worst of all.

Minutes passed where I sat with tears flowing freely. I didn't bother wiping them or trying to stop. My soul was releasing the feelings I was burying in the form of tears. Each drop lifted a little burden and shed a little light. Before things got worse, I had to formulate a plan to make it better. If not for me, for my daughter.

"Shiiiiit," I cried out after the intense pain had returned.

After waiting for the pain to subside once again, I tried to stand; and that's when it happened.

"No, it's too soon." I sniffled back tears, realizing my water had broken.

CHAPTER TEN

Quest

*T*oday, I'm taking one of the biggest L's of my tenure in the streets, and all I keep telling myself is it could be worse. That's something niggas tell themselves when they were trying to make themselves feel better about how bad shit had gotten for them. I've never been in the position I found myself in now, and it fucking sucks.

"Are you okay?" I glanced back and looked up at Aubri who was leaning against the frame of our walk-in closet.

"I'm good, bae. Tired of going through this fucking money."

A nigga was sitting on the floor of the closet, Indian style, packing stacks of hundreds into a suitcase on wheels.

"Cross and Quavo here. I told them I would come up and get you. I'm about to shower and get dressed. Ashlynn is coming over and we are going to pick up Milani and have a little girls' day out."

"Aight, I'm just about done in here. When you leave, come in here and take some bread."

"I'm good on that, Quest. Whatever you are going out to do today, be careful. I love you."

"Always. I love you too."

I could hear Aubri's footsteps get further away as I tossed the last few stacks of money into the suitcase. After zipping it up, I rose to my feet and lugged it downstairs to the living room where Qua and Cross were waiting.

"What's good?" I greeted them.

"You sound sad; must be feeling how I'm feeling?" Cross attempted to joke.

Hell yeah I was fucking sad. I was putting up 2.5 million of my own money to pay Julio back and get an advance shipment. Cross was definitely feeling the burn too because in the suitcase near his foot, was the 2.5 he was putting up to cover our complete loss. It was a minor setback, but a setback nonetheless.

Quavo raised his hand like a student before speaking. "Y'all could cheer up a little. I been on my shit and already secured new routes. So, as soon as y'all secure the product, it can go out. Meeko got the trucks ready, the maps of the new routes at the spot. Everything on my end is covered."

"Impressive, Qua."

Always made sure I gave credit where credit was due. Quavo stepped up and was coming through in a major way, and I had to figure out a way to thank him. A way other than just telling him. Sometimes that wasn't enough when a nigga was showing how much he was willing to ride for you.

"We owe you, Quavo," Cross said, speaking my thoughts. "You really came through for us in the clutch."

"Just looking out for family."

Glancing down out my watch, I realized Cross and I had to leave right then, if we were going to make it to Julio on time. If we were late, we could kiss the advance shipment goodbye for sure.

"Yo, we really gotta get up out of here."

Cross nodded while digging in his pockets. He pulled out his keys and tossed them over to Quavo.

"Take care of my baby. I'll call you when we on our way back here so you can pick me up."

Qua agreed to Cross's terms, and together we left; Quavo, to do whatever it is he was going to do, and Cross and I, to handle shit with Julio. We pulled up to the meeting spot with three minutes to spare. As expected, Julio and his men were already there. After killing the engine, Cross and I emerged from the whip. While I approached Julio and his men, Cross grabbed the suitcases out the trunk.

"Had me worried there. Thought you weren't going to show," Julio spoke as I was being patted down by one of his men.

"By now, you have to know me better than that."

"I thought I did," Julio said solemnly. "What's going on? You know I have a flight to catch."

By this time, Cross had joined us and was getting searched.

"Here's the five million for the last shipment. On time, as always."

"Oh?" He looked surprised.

"Don't be so surprised. For the first time in a while, we ran into a little hiccup, but it wasn't nothing we couldn't solve. We do, however, need our next shipment expedited."

Julio laughed while rubbing his hands together. He snapped and the two men who were standing beside him took the cases from Cross's side and carried them over to the truck they arrived in.

"I heard all about this little hiccup as you called it. It was a good time for me to test and see how y'all would handle a situation like this, seeing as we've never been in one like this together. I appreciate you taking care of whatever necessary to get my money on time and not coming to me with excuses. Job well done. Because I trusted the type of men you both are, I already put things in motion for you. The next shipment was just waiting on y'all to make a move."

Everything was a test with Julio. Good thing we weren't dumb niggas and passed them all with flying colors.

"Things like this happen. It's how we deal with it that determines the kind of businessmen you are. Again, you two show me that I'm betting on the right horse. I hope you figure out how that little hiccup happened. It's unfortunate, but again, things like this happen."

"It's all good, boss," one of his men whispered to him, in reference to the money we gave him.

"Well good. I can have the product ready tomorrow. Are your trucks secure? New routes?"

"We took care of all of that," Cross answered.

"Good. We're done here. As always, it's good doing business with you."

Cross and I waited for Julio and his men to leave before jumping back in my whip and getting low. Meeting didn't go as we expected because Julio was calm and cool about the whole thing. But we had product coming in, and that's what was most important. We lived to see another day in the business.

Ashlynn

After dropping CJ off to his grandmother, I was going to enjoy a much-needed girls' day with Aubri and Milani. It would be the first time meeting Milani, and I was excited and anxious to see Aubri in mommy mode, if that's what you would call it. She hated when I referred to her as a mom, but she was, regardless of the circumstances. I had a great feeling about today. It's already something special about the way Aubri lights up whenever she mentions Milani to me, so I can only imagine what it would be like witnessing their interactions in person. Pulling up in front of Quest's place, I knew he was with Cross and they were somewhere handling business, so I didn't see the need to go in when we'd only be leaving right back out.

"Call, Aubs," I instructed my car.

She answered on the first ring. "I saw when you pulled up, I'm coming out now." When I looked up, there she was making her way down the driveway toward my car.

Once the call ended, I put the car in park, grabbed my bag and got out. We were taking Aubri's car. Mainly because she had to go and pick Milani up, and if we're being honest; I didn't feel like driving. The start to our ride was a little silent beside the Fab mixtape she had playing. That was unusual for us, but I figured she was nervous being that it was the first time she was bringing her daughter around anyone but Quest.

"How are you enjoying getting to know Milani?"

"Honestly, I thought she would resent me and we'd never get in a good space, but things are going better than I expected. We're learning each other, and it's just crazy how much we have in common," Aubri answered. Again, her face lit up and she had this twinkle in her eye.

"You ever noticed whenever Milani's mentioned, your whole face lights up?" I asked, loving this new side of Aubri I've been seeing since Milani came around.

"No, and it's crazy because Quest said the same thing to me. I just hope I'm not coming off as I'm trying too hard or doing too much to her," Aubri admitted.

"From what I've been witnessing from a distance, you're doing everything right, so far. I'm proud of you. Just remember, she's a newly teenaged girl, and she's at that age where they began to go through changes and develop that bad attitude; get prepared," I let her know.

"Thanks, Ash, that means a lot coming from you. And I'm already mentally preparing myself for that. Just hope it's not as bad as the horror stories I've heard from other parents," Aubri stated while shaking her head.

"Girl, for some reason, I can't shake the feeling that I'm being watched," I said changing the subject.

"Probably just paranoid. I mean, look who's your husband, why would you be? I be having that feeling too sometimes, but that's also because I overthink every little thing. Girl, better buy a gun and start going to the gun range so you can be prepared to let off a few solid rounds if you have to," Aubri joked, as she came to a complete stop in front of an apartment building.

"That might not be a bad idea." I nodded, liking her suggestion.

She was too busy on her phone to hear me agree with her. When a smile spread across her face, I turned toward the window next to me and saw a little Aubri approaching the car.

"Girl! That is your child," I squealed.

Hearing about Milani was one thing, but seeing the little lady in the flesh was another. I was literally looking at thirteen-year-old, Aubri. The closer she got, the clearer the resemblance came. She even walked like her. Bourgeois as hell.

The back door to the car opened and Milani climbed in.

"Hiiiii." She seemed just as excited as Aubri.

"Hola, lovely. This is Ashlynn. Ashy, this is Milani."

I turned around as far as I could in my seat to greet her.

"It's so nice to meet you, Milani."

She leaned forward and hugged me from behind.

"Same here."

She seemed sweet.

"So, Aubri already warned me that it's your world and we're just chauffeuring you around. So where to first?"

"Well, I'm starving."

Giggling to myself, I had to grin at Aubri. That was an Aubri trait for sure. Always wanted to eat.

"Food it is."

Grabbing lunch was the start to an amazing day out. We ended up going to the spa for massages and facials, did some light shopping, and even caught a movie. It was still early in the game, but I could tell Milani was going to be a great addition to our ladies' circle. We may have had to change up some of the things we liked to do, mainly drink, and swap it for some teenage activities, but my new little sweetie was worth it. With all that we'd been going through lately, spending the day with Milani was a nice change of pace and had me looking forward to our next day out before the one we were having was even over.

CHAPTER ELEVEN

Aubri

*W*ho would have thought I would have loved working in real estate so much? Working for Ashlynn was the best, and it wasn't because we were close. She didn't give me special privileges at work because of our relationship, she was just a dope ass boss. The job was amazing, the people were fun to work with once they got used to me being around, and the pay was great. I appreciated that above anything else. As long as I did what I was supposed to do, I made enough to continue paying for my grandmother's care, the rent at the apartment I never went to, and tossed Quest money to put toward his home since I stayed there now. Well, I tried to. He never took money from me. Most of the time, I would have to slip bills in his wallet with the money he already had. He would always figure it out but knew I wouldn't take it back, so he didn't try. In addition to work, I still was able to relieve my stresses by going to the gun range every Monday with Ashlynn. That had become one of my favorite pastimes. It was just something about it that made me feel in control when I was losing control in other aspects in my life.

My daughter. This bright, witty, even slightly sarcastic, thirteen-year-old, showed me a whole new world. It got to the point where I'd be in the office on Monday morning, after taking her to school, looking forward to Friday when she'd be coming over to spend a few hours. She didn't spend a night, yet, but I was okay with that because we talked all the time. Quest and I took turns, taking her to and from school. Well, we alternated with Stephanie. She spent time with the whole gang; even CJ had fallen in love with her.

"Someone is here for you," Quest spoke from the entryway of the kitchen. I looked up, and there he was standing with Milani. He had gone to pick her up from school while I got started on lunch.

"Milani!" I walked around the counter to where they stood and gave her a hug. "How was school?" I asked her.

"It was good. What you made? Not grass I hope," she joked.

"I'm a take your bag up to the room," Quest said before leaving Milani and I alone in the kitchen. It was her first time staying over and just couldn't contain my excitement.

"Real funny, but no. Quest requested steak, asparagus, and a baked potato for you animal killers," I told her.

"Yesss. Ten points for Quest."

We laughed before I instructed her to wash her hands.

"You shall help me set the table."

This was all new to me. I would make my and Quest's plates and we would sit in front of the TV. I wanted to try something different. The normal family dynamic that I haven't had the chance to experience in years. I wanted to experience that with my kid.

"Aubri, we don't have to sit at the table. In my house, we eat in front of the TV or in our room, or whatever."

"My type of girl." Quest made his presence known as he walked back into the kitchen.

"That's cool with me. In the living room, it is."

"Good, so we can watch *SportsCenter*," Milani stated.

I tossed my hands up not believing I had another sports person on my hands.

"Not you too," I pretended to whine.

Quest slapped her high five and laughed. "Yes, you too," he added.

They chopped it up about their favorite sports teams while I made our plates. That's when they finally decided to pay me attention and helped me into the living room with the food. Milani was in charge of bringing our waters.

"You play sports?" Quest asked, Milani.

"I run track, but I'm thinking about trying out for girls' varsity this year."

"Basketball?" I inquired.

She nodded while digging into her food.

"That's what's up. When you make the team, let us know. We'll definitely pop up out to your games and support. Get some Team Milani shirts made and shit."

She laughed and covered her face.

"How embarrassing. Oh my God. But I'll definitely let you guys know. I'm not sure because I have to go by my dance and track schedule."

"Yeah, don't spread yourself too thin. You gotta stay on top of your grades too," Quest told her.

I was so into stuffing my face with a salad I made for myself, but I was listening to them.

Quest's phone rung and he did something he never did; he took it and left the room.

"You really into these sports highlights, girl?"

She nodded.

"I missed the game last night because I was studying."

"Ahh, okay. Well, carry on."

The damn sports announcers were so animated that they even sucked me into the TV.

"I'm so sorry. But I gotta run out," Quest announced. "I'll make it up to you, Milani. Babe, we'll talk later."

"No need for apologies, Quest. Y'all got me all weekend. We'll kick it tomorrow."

Milani may not have wanted an explanation or apology, but I did. Quest knew how important this weekend was to me, so I wanted to know what was more important. I didn't even have a chance to respond because after Milani said what she said, he left. I tried focusing on the TV, but my thoughts wandered to what he ran out for. That didn't last long though, because thanks to the itis, Milani and I both passed out on the couch.

Quest

*H*ated that I had to dip out on Milani and Aubri the way I did, but I had to make it to the hospital. It wasn't even about Lia. If her little shorty was mine, I had to be there. Aubri would definitely understand had it turned out to be the case. I made it to Methodist in record breaking time, considering I had to stop at Babies "R" Us to get a car seat. After going through the hospital's sign-in procedures, I was finally directed to Lia's room. Walking in, I found her alone, bawling her eyes out.

"Fuck are you crying for?" I questioned, gaining her attention.

"So much is…"

Before she got to all that, I needed that good ol' DNA test done. If shorty wasn't mine, I was out. She could keep the car seat.

"Wait, Li. Before we start chopping it up like old friends, can you get the doctor in here to take my blood or whatever they gotta do."

She rolled her eyes and sucked her teeth. That shit made me no never mind. She already knew what type time I was on, so I hope she wasn't expecting anything different. She reached for the cord beside her and pressed the button as I took a seat on the chair near the window.

"Decent ass hospital," I spoke while observing her room. "You went in labor alone?"

She nodded, but remained silent.

"Damn, that had to suck."

"It did. She was a few weeks early and underweight. But she's good now. You not going to ask to see her."

"No," I stated, flatly.

Lia knew I wasn't one to sugarcoat shit. I didn't want to see the baby and get all attached if she wasn't my seed. When the results came back and if she was mine, of course I would want to see her. But until then, nope.

"Ms. Perkins, you called for me?" A nurse walked in and headed straight to Lia's bedside.

Lia turned her head toward me and pointed.

"He's here. Remember I told you and Dr. Alston about the blood test."

"Yep. Let me get everything set up and we'll get that taken care of."

The nurse walked out the room, leaving me and Lia in silence. She looked as if so much was on her mind to say, but she was holding it in because she knew I didn't want to converse with her until after the results. The nurse returned with what I assumed was a DNA testing kit. I thought she was going to take blood, but instead, she just did a cheek swab.

"Okay, that's all. You'll have the results in one to two days. Because of the circumstance, the results will be rushed."

"One day?" I looked to Lia.

"Yes, will that be a problem?"

"Nah, that's fine."

I thanked the nurse and watched as she went on her way.

"So, do you want to see her now?"

"No." My answer wasn't going to change.

"Call me in one or two days when you get the results."

"Quest, you know what—"

She was mid-sentence and I was already at the door ready to dip.

"Thanks for the car seat," she muttered. "I heard about your shipment."

Now she had my undivided attention.

"Oh yeah? How?"

She shrugged and turned over.

"Lia, you know me well enough to know I don't play about my money. You really wanna play this game?"

Hopefully, she didn't take my threat lightly. When she slowly turned back over to face me, I knew she was taking me serious.

"Streets talk, Quest. You out of everyone should know you can't keep everyone on your team happy."

"That's funny, Li, 'cause I'm almost certain we don't walk the same streets."

"Well then MY streets are saying Trey had something to do with it."

"Yeah, nah. I'm not entertaining you."

Before she could respond, I dipped. My mouth said one thing to her, but my gut was saying something else. I'd be a fool not to look into such an accusation, but an even bigger fool if I played this the wrong way and lost a good worker in the process. Being who I am, I was going to look into it right away. When I made it back to my car, I called Aubri to fill her in, then I hit Cross and Quavo and told them to meet me at the spot and have Trey meet us there too. I specifically told them to let him go alone and I'd meet them outside. I been in this game for so long, I had a different way to play it down pat.

<>

When I pulled up to the spot, I spotted Quavo and Cross sitting in Cross's parked whip. I killed the engine to mine, got out, and went over to his. When they spotted me, Cross unlocked the door and I jumped in the back.

"What happened?" Cross got right down to it.

"I don't want to believe it, but shit happens," I started to explain.

Quavo turned around in his seat and looked at me oddly.

"What happened, Q?" he inquired.

"Did Trey show up, yet?"

Quavo nodded.

"Listen, I don't know how true it is. But apparently, Trey's the one who called the DEA and got the shipment intercepted."

"Fuck outta here," Cross groaned.

Quavo sat there, shaking his head.

"That shit don't make no sense. What would he get out of that?" Cross added.

"I'm not saying he did or he didn't. I'm saying what was told to me.

We here to see what information he'll offer us after a little motivation."

"So, let's go then."

Before I could say anything else, Cross was climbing out the car. Quavo wasn't far behind. By the time I joined them, Cross was already banging on the door, yelling for Trey to open it.

"Y'all niggas ran up here like some shit wen—"

Trey's sentence was cut off by the blow I delivered to his midsection that sent him flying backwards. Quavo and Cross watched on astonished at how I went straight to one hundred. The only reason I didn't pull out my piece was because I wasn't sure how good Lia's intel was. But I knew how to get a nigga to tell on himself, if there was anything to tell. So I had to get Trey where I wanted him.

"Fuck is wrong with you, Q?" he wailed, while lying on his back, gripping his stomach.

By this time, Quavo had walked over to his side. I thought he was gonna help the nigga but even he was on the fence about Trey's loyalty after what I told them. Cross wasn't on the same time as I was. That nigga had his piece out, resting it right in front of him, ready to blow Trey's head off if it came down to it.

"I think we treat y'all well. Don't we, Quavo?"

I looked over to Quavo who was still staring down at Trey as if he was trying to figure him out.

"Quavo!" I barked to get his attention.

"Yeah, yeah. My bad. Y'all treat us better than well, Q. We eat like y'all eat. Nigga's don't treat us like workers. Y'all respect us how y'all respect each other," he explained without taking his eyes off of Trey.

"Yeah, that's what I thought too."

Drawing my foot back then swinging it forward, I kicked Trey in the side like I was a football player kicking for the one extra point after a touchdown. His cry sounded painful and ugly as fuck.

"Shut the fuck up," Cross spat.

Leaning over, I grabbed him by his shirt and yanked him forward, causing his head to jerk. Then unexpectedly, slammed it against the floor.

"Ouchhhh," Cross squealed.

The sound of his head coming in contact with the floor made a loud thud sound. His eyes rolled in the back of his head but didn't close. To be sure, I slapped him twice.

Whap, whap!

"Good, good. Don't pass on me, Trey."

"Q. Q. Q!"

I don't know if it was the shock of having his head slammed against the floor or his nerves, but the nigga couldn't get a sentence out.

"See, I'm offended, Trey. And you should know better than to offend me. I treated you well, and you repay me by stealing my money."

He wasn't in this predicament for talking. I was looking for a certain reaction and he gave it to me when his eyes nearly popped out of his head when I mentioned him stealing.

"I… never stole fro—from you, Q."

Cross stepped up and aimed his gun at his head.

"Oh, so I'm a liar?" Cross taunted Trey while waving his gun around.

Frantically, Trey shook his head no.

"I… never to—to—took money. The ni—He… He had, he… Call the DEA. I. I. I. not money."

And there it was. A little ass whooping and the nigga told on himself.

"You cost us five million fucking dollars. FIVE MILLION!"

Reaching up, I grabbed Cross's gun and quickly brought it down, slamming it against his head. Spit spewed from his mouth causing me to jump back.

"Who you working with or for?" Cross asked him calmly.

Trey's eyes rolled again. This time it took him a little longer to open them.

"He ne—never, said hi- hi- his name," he slurred.

None of us could contain the laugh we let out simultaneously. Quavo backed out his pistol and aimed.

"You snaked your guys for a nigga that couldn't even tell you his name. When you see that nigga in hell, make sure you get it."

Taking Cross and I by surprise, he pulled back on the trigger twice for good measure, though the first shot through the center of his forehead did the trick.

"Scum ass bitch," Quavo spat. "I got the clean up on this one. Nigga ain't having no funeral, I'ma dissolve him. Y'all sticking around for that?"

"Oh, nah, do your thing," I told Qua. I done seem blood, guts, brain matter, and all that crazy shit, but no way was I sticking around to watch a nigga body dissolve into liquid.

Cross shook his head. "I'm good on that too. Call the guys and let 'em know to come back you up."

"Bet. I'll call when I take the trash out."

"Say less."

Cross and I didn't waste a minute getting up out of there. I know we were thinking the same thing, but like the many other crimes we committed together, it was already done so there was no need to discuss it.

CHAPTER TWELVE

Cross

*F*inally, shit was settling. The shipment getting intercepted was the last real problem Quest and I faced. It seemed like once Trey disappeared, so did all our problems. I still couldn't believe the nigga greased us, but nowadays, you just couldn't put shit past anyone, and he proved that. All bullshit aside, business was booming. Using the trucks to distribute was a genius idea. It got the work off the quickest; less risks for me and Quest. Even though shit on the business front was good, it didn't take away from my plans on going legit. I just couldn't do that as soon as I wanted to. This was a new realm for Quest and myself, and I wasn't going to leave him to explore it alone until I was confident that he didn't need me. So, business was still business, but the importance of family was even more evident in my life.

Ash and I were good. Great even. Some nights, we would lie in bed and she would break down crying, telling me how bad I hurt her, but how she loved me much deeper than the hurt I caused to her. That shit did something to me. I knew for the rest of my life, I'd be aiming to make up for what I did to my family, but I didn't care. Whatever it took, I was willing to do. My world didn't make sense without Ashlynn, so if she wanted me to jump through hoops while balancing tennis balls on my head, I would join the circus for practice. I wasn't the only one readjusting to family life.

Quest found himself reevaluating life and family too. With Milani in the picture, I could tell he was starting to question a lot of shit too. She wasn't his daughter, but I could tell he cared about her, and because of that, he knew he needed to make changes. Regardless of your profession or whatever path you decided to take in life, it changes the moment you have human beings who depended on you. Milani had her adopted mother, but she had us too. Quest wouldn't hesitate to be there for her if she needed because of what she meant to Aubri. And since she and Aubri were working on building a mother-daughter like relationship, he knew he had to be a better example for her. I couldn't even front, my nigga was good at the parenting thing. The more Milani came around, the softer Quest became. She might as well had been his seed because her presence had the same effect on him as a daughter would her father. Nigga was like putty for Milani and Aubri, as it should have been because they were his family.

After years in this game, I knew that shit only stayed good for but so long. However, I had all intentions on enjoying the calm before the next storm.

Ashlynn

For a minute, I just stood watching him jump up and down on the bed with excitement. Normally, I would have told his narrow ass to take a seat, but I, too, shared his joy. It'd been a journey to say the least, in terms of me and Cross getting back on track with our marriage. Today, I was happy to say that we were in a really good place. A great place, actually. That's not why CJ was excited though, because it was still unknown to him that his dad and I were ever going through a tumultuous time. He was excited because the Disney trip we had been planning for so long was finally happening.

"Okay, boy. Get down and put on your clothes, unless you want me and Daddy to go without you."

Hearing that we would leave him, caused CJ to stop jumping instantly. He flopped down on his butt then slid off the bed onto his feet.

"I thought that would bring you back from your little zone. But hurry and get dressed."

"Okay, Mommy."

After watching him for another minute, I turned and headed back downstairs just as someone started ringing the bell. Although I already knew who it was, I peered through the glass to check, for obvious reasons.

"Look who's early," I sang out while opening the door for Aubri. To my surprise, she was accompanied by Milani.

"What a surprise. My boo!" I squealed before going around Aubri and pulling Milani in for a hug.

"Wow. I'm the one driving y'all asses to the airport, and she's the one that gets all the love."

"Don't even hate. Heyyy, Auntie. Where's CJ?"

"Upstairs. If you are going up there to see him, make sure his ass is getting dressed."

"I got you," Milani assured me before taking the steps up to CJ's room.

Once I was sure she was out of earshot, I turned to Aubri and smiled. "Auntie? We there?" I questioned. Milani had been coming around more and more, but I hadn't heard her to refer to Aubri as mom, or me as auntie, Cross as uncle, none of that. Aubri didn't seem shocked.

"I know, right. It's new. She asked me if she could call you and Cross auntie and uncle. She likes being around y'all. She even slipped up and called me Ma, once or twice. Mostly Aubri still, but just knowing that she sees me as her mom, even though we are so close in age and I haven't been there, makes me have hope."

That's where I had to stop her.

"Please, let's not even go there. The past is the past, Aub. Since she's come back into your life, you have been there. We all have been, so of course she's adjusting to having her extended family. And y'all may be close in age, but Milani knows you'll get in that ass if she gets crazy, as a mom would. Or shit, I will do it for you."

174

We laughed while heading into the living room.

"Fortunately, we don't have those problems."

"Well good. So, besides that, what's been up?"

"Nothing you need to worry yourself about when you about to go on a family trip."

Because I knew Aubri, I knew better than to try to pry whatever was on her mind out of her. I'd just have to wait 'til I got back to discuss it.

"Girls' day when I get back?"

She nodded and smiled.

"Where Cross? Y'all ready, or y'all trying to miss y'all flight."

"Your ass is early."

Aubri sat down on the couch and crossed one leg over the other before looking up at me sideways.

"You acting like it's not gonna take you forever to get through TSA."

"That's true. Let me get these boys."

Aubri rose to her feet and sauntered over to where our bags were against the wall, before she walked out of the living room.

"I'll start taking these to the car."

"Okay, thank you. Leave Cross's duffel. His ass can carry that shit."

"Alright."

Aubri grabbed my and CJ's spinner luggage and headed for the door while I headed upstairs to get the boys. Cross was already ready;

it was CJ that I was worried about. However, Milani had him together. They were sitting on his bed playing the Nintendo Wii.

"We out. Lani, take him to the car while I get his father."

"Okay. Come on, big boy," she instructed CJ.

To my knowledge, Milani never had any siblings from her adopted mom, and she didn't from Aubri, so when she met CJ, she really bonded with him and treated him as if he were her little brother. I just loved their little relationship.

"Ready, boo?" I asked Cross from the door of our bedroom.

He glanced over at me, briefly taking his eyes off ESPN, and smiled before giving the TV his attention, this time to turn it off.

"Yep. We taking Uber?"

Shaking my head, no, I made my way over to him as he got off the bed. "Nope. Aubri showed up and she brought Milani with her."

"I'm shocked. I just knew her ass was going to oversleep."

"And she was early," I added.

Standing toe to toe, Cross reached his arm around me and palmed my ass, using his grip to pull me into him. After a moment of staring into each other's eyes, our lips met.

"I love you," he mumbled through our kiss.

"I love you too, baby. Let's go roast in Florida and make sure our boy has the best vacation ever."

"Wouldn't have it any other way."

Grabbing his hand, I led the way out of the bedroom, not before grabbing my bag off the dresser. Before going downstairs, I peeked into CJ's room, to find that he and Milani had already went down, but his iPad was on the dresser so I grabbed it for him. My son would have lost his shit if he had to sit on a plane for three hours without his entertainment.

"Aubri took me and CJ's bags to the car. Get yours out the living room."

Leaving Cross to fetch his bag, I headed outside. Milani was chasing CJ around the yard, and Aubri was sitting in the driver's seat with the window rolled down. She had her elbow perched up on the window and was leaning out, laughing at Milani and CJ.

"You got everything, Ashy?" Cross called from the front door.

Turning toward him, I paused and did a mental check. After assuring myself that I had everything, I told him yeah. He turned to lock the door. Hearing a car pull up and come to a complete stop caught my attention. At first I paid it no mind, but after seeing the look on Aubri's face, I had to turn to see who was stepping out of the car.

"What the fuck are you doing here?" I roared.

Watching her close her door to the cab and walk over to the back door on the other side, angered me. I could literally feel the boiling blood sensation in my body. I hadn't seen this girl since I decked her bitch ass during our little lunch, which was months ago; but this was still too soon. As if showing up at my crib unannounced wasn't enough...

"Yo, Lia, what—" Cross's words were shoved back into his mouth as she leaned over and pulled a car seat out the back of the car.

"Nah," I whispered while shaking my head.

I didn't even notice Aubri getting out of the truck, but she ended up by my side, pulling me in the opposite direction of Lia and her baby.

"Let me go, Aubri," I insisted.

"Nah, Ash. Let Cross speak to her. CJ out here. He definitely don't need to see this go left."

She knew something that she wasn't telling me, and it only pissed me off even more.

"What aren't you telling me?" I spun out of her embrace and yelled in Cross's direction. "That's your baby?"

He tossed his hands up and cautiously walked toward me. Lia stood there, car seat in hand not saying a word. I swear if she didn't have that baby in her hand I would have knocked that smug ass look right off her fucking face.

"Ash, take CJ in the back in the house."

"Nah. What's up? What she here for? Am I the only one not privy to some sick ass joke?"

Cross tossed Milani the keys to the house.

"Take him in the house," he instructed. "Lia?"

Finally, she spoke up. "I'm not here for drama. I swear to you, I'm not even on that type of time."

"So why are you here? Get to the point," I barked.

"Cross." She looked away from me to him. "I need you to take her. I can't get into the details right now, but I can't keep her with me and…"

Cross stepped in her direction.

"And what?"

"You're her father."

Didn't see that train coming until it smacked dead into me. All the air escaped my body, and I gasped at an attempt to take in oxygen. My legs felt feeble and wobbled freely beneath me. If it wasn't for Aubri standing right here holding me up, I probably would have hit the ground. I don't know what was killing me more; her revelation, or the fact that Cross didn't object or question her. It was like he knew. Did he?

"Cr—Cross." Getting his name out took air and energy that I just didn't have. My cheeks were damp due to the tears I hadn't noticed flowing, until one landed above my lip. My stomach was turning, and a visible pain was felt in my chest. "How are you so sure that he's the father?" I managed to get out.

Neither she nor Cross bothered to answer me. Instead, they stood there, now toe to toe, having an intense stare down.

"Quest took a DNA test," Aubri mumbled more to herself than to anyone else, but I heard her.

My head snapped in her direction. "And you didn't tell me? You knew too, Cross?" Stalking over to him, I pushed him, forcing him out of the trance he was in. "You knew the baby could have been yours and you didn't tell me? You knew Quest got tested?"

"I didn't know shit, man." Cross finally opened his mouth and used his words.

"Aubri, how? Why?"

She shook her head and offered an apology. I don't know why I felt betrayed by her; at the end of the day, she didn't owe me anything. I just thought girl code meant something.

"Cross, I can't stay here much longer. Please, just take her. I swear if I could have avoided this I would have. When Quest came out not to be her dad, I wasn't even going to bother you. Was willing and able to do it on my own."

"What changed?"

"I just can't," Lia spoke while pleading with her eyes. She glanced down at the baby for a minute before passing her over to Cross. "I'm sorry, Ashlynn," she admitted as she backed away.

Cross called after her. "Li, if you leave her here, don't come back."

Lia nodded. "Take care of our girl."

Wham!

A huge slap across the face. My husband, the man I vowed to give all of me to for as long as I lived, had another girl… more so another girl, a baby; and she wasn't mine. We all watched as Lia climbed back in the cab and it drove off, before Cross turned to me and took steps forward.

"How could you?" I questioned.

He shrugged. "What? How could I what? What the fuck was I supposed to say?"

"So, I don't matter? You don't think this is something we needed to discuss first? Something I needed to process? You just think I'm willing and able to jump into stepmother mode? That's selfish as fuck."

"Ash, you know I would never wish this shit to happen to us, ma. But it did. I'm sorry, you know that. I worked my ass off to get us back to this place; you think I wanted this? But it is happening. You not gonna make me choose between you and my daughter."

"What if I did?" Regardless of how I felt, I would never seriously ask him to make that decision, but for the fuck of it, I wanted to know what he would say.

"Trust me. You don't want to do that."

Without another word, he walked around me with the car seat in his hand and headed into the house. Aubri went to say something but I deaded that.

"You can leave. I'll send Milani out."

Cross

*H*earing Milani say bye to Ashlynn and the door slam behind her, forced me to open my eyes. I don't know why, but for the moment, I sat with my eyes closed; I wished like hell that when I opened them, this shit would have been a bad ass dream. I wasn't so lucky though. As I opened my eyes and glanced down, I stared at the baby sleeping peacefully. Something told me to look toward the entrance of the living room, and there stood Ashlynn staring back at me.

"So what now?" I asked her.

Heartbreak radiated off her. A little while ago, her eyes were so full of life. Her skin was glowing and everything just seemed good. The Ashy standing there was the complete opposite in all aspects. I don't know what I expected from her, but I needed to know how we were moving forward.

"Congratulations," she uttered sarcastically.

Didn't even bother to address that. I deserved whatever cheap shots she was going to take at me. The part that had me fucked up was that Quest didn't tell me he had a DNA test done. Even though, after he told me Lia was pregnant, I still didn't allow myself to believe that I could possibly be the father; I still expected him to tell me. Granted, we did have a lot of shit going on, but you make time for what you want. Nigga could have easily slipped that somewhere in one of our conversations.

In that moment, all I could think about was Lyfe Jennings song "Must Be Nice." *"Even when those hustling days are gone, she'll be by your side still holding on. Even when those twenties stop spinning, and all those gold-digging women disappear, she'll still be here."* That hook rang true for Ashlynn and the type of wife she'd been to me. But I knew for a fact a baby wasn't included in that. To be honest, as much as I loved her and my family, I wasn't going to fix my lips to ask her to stay after this. It would be the most selfish thing to do to the woman I loved, and I wasn't going to. If she did stay, and I hoped like hell she did, it would be because she wanted to, not because I coerced her to.

"Ash, here me out," I started. She took a few steps toward me, sniffled back tears, then continued, and took a seat on the couch across from me.

"CJ's trip."

"I'll make it up to him."

"No. Aubri put our stuff in the yard. I'm going to call an Uber and I'm going to take him to Disney. He's not going to keep suffering because of your actions, Cross. It's not fair."

"Ash."

She held her hand up. "It's not up for discussion."

And with that, she rose from her seat and left me sitting there. As soon as she walked out of the living room, the baby started stirring, making a fuss. Leaning over, I picked her up and rocked her gently. Staring down at her, I searched for the slightest sign of CJ or myself. It was hard because besides our complexion, she was all Lia.

"Damn!" The door slammed shut once again, meaning that

Ashlynn and CJ left without saying bye. The sound startled little mama because she was back to fussing. "It's aight, little pea. It's okay."

What the fuck was I going to do with a baby? Sad shit, I didn't even know her name. After twenty minutes of rocking and rapping "A Boogie," she was knocked out. I placed her back in the car seat, dug into my pocket, and pulled out my phone to shoot Quest a text.

Come to the crib, as soon as you can.

A full minute ain't even go by before his reply came through.

Q: Aubri already put me on. En route.

Quest

After tossing my phone back over to the passenger seat, I eased my foot off the brake since the light had changed back to green. I was headed to one of my spots to check on some shit when Aubri called me telling me what Lia pulled. I figured Cross would need me, whether it was to referee between him and Ashlynn or just to be there, so I was already on my way when he texted me. Just when I thought Lia couldn't get any lower, she up and did. Who just drops their child off with somebody with no explanation? I don't care if it's the baby's father or not. I felt for Cross, though. He had to deal with shorty for eighteen years, and on top of that, he had to deal with his wife. This was indeed his karma, though.

When I pulled up to the crib, I opted to park on the street versus the driveway, since the spot was empty. After killing the engine to my whip, I climbed out and made my way up to the front door. Didn't even get a chance to ring the bell.

"Damn, you were peeking through the window?" I asked while walking into the house.

Quest was holding the baby against his chest with one arm, bouncing her up and down.

"You trying to give her shaking syndrome, my nigga?"

I didn't have kids, but I knew he was bouncing her a little too fast.

"Son, she don't stop crying. Chill, little pea. Life ain't that rough for you yet."

"Little pea?" I repeated while laughing.

Crossed brushed me off and walked back into the living room. "What the fuck I'm supposed to call her. Lia ain't even tell me her name."

Not that I would do any better at soothing shorty than be was doing, but I could tell he was about to completely lose his shit, so I reached out and took her from him.

"Raelyn, it's iight. Ya pops ain't have to do this shit in a few years; he rusty."

Cross's neck twisted in my direction and his brow raised. He was probably wondering how I knew her name.

"Lia said it when she hit me to take the DNA test," I told him before he could ask.

"About that. Why you didn't give me a heads up, son?"

"Nigga, I did. I told you she was pregnant and I told you, you smashed as well as I did. You chose not to take the shit seriously. Plus, after I found out, we had to take care of the shit with Trey so it completely slipped my mind."

"She picked the wrong time to do this shit. Nigga was literally on the lawn about to jump in the car and head to the airport, then here she come. What the fuck am I supposed to do?"

The way he was panicking really made me laugh. This wasn't his first time to the parenting rodeo, so he was just being extra as hell.

"You have a kid already, bro. Why you acting like you never did this before? The process to changing diapers ain't change. You know to feed her and shit. Relax."

He started pacing and huffing like he was trying to catch his breath. I swear you only see this type of shit in the movies.

"Cross, relax," I barked.

Raelynn jumped from me screaming and started crying again.

"My bad, princess. Ya pops an idiot, had to bark on him really quick," I whispered to the baby while gently rubbing her back to soothe her.

"It's not about taking care of her. Of course, I can do that part. My wife, son. You know how bad Ashlynn wanted another baby. But not like this, bro. I can't expect her to stick around for this. This little girl changes everything."

Guilt consumed me. I thought of everything except how this was going to tear Ashlynn apart. I felt for her. Ash was a good ass wife to Cross, and she ain't deserve this shit in the least bit. At the same time, I knew her.

"She loves you. Raelynn is a part of you. I'll bet money on the fact that Ash will learn to love her too. It's not going to happen overnight and it won't be easy, but she will. And you right, don't ask her to stay, don't expect her to stay; just let her know that you need her and that you understand how this shit is affecting her, so whatever she decides, you won't argue. Put the ball in her court and just work at being the best father you can to your kids. Shit with Ash will work itself out."

"When did you become the expert?" Cross questioned

sarcastically.

"Fuck you. Nigga, take my free advice or go pay one of them niggas to lay on their black couch and tell them your problems. Make all the jokes you want; you know I'm right."

"That was the door?" Cross looked to me.

"Yeah, you want me to get?"

He nodded and took the baby from me. I got up and headed back to the front to get the door. To my fucking surprise, Lia was on the other side. Shorty had big balls today, and she was letting them all hang out.

"Let me get Cross," I told her before she had a chance to speak.

"Quest."

Holding up my hand up, I stopped her, before calling out for Cross. "Yo, Cross! Li, shorty ain't mine so we have nothing to discuss."

"I told you not to fucking come back here," Cross roared.

I looked back at him and he didn't have Raelynn.

"Nigga, where the baby?"

"In the living room, knocked out in her car seat. Why you here?"

Lia took a step forward.

"Stay right there," Cross instructed her.

She dropped the bag she was holding at my feet.

"That's everything for Raelynn. Her birth certificate and every other important document you may need. I'm sorry. I am truly sorry for everything I've done to the both you. I love my daughter, our daughter, and that's why I'm leaving her here. I know you won't let anything happen to her, Cross. I'm leaving to save my life, and I just don't want to involve her. Please, just let her know her mom loves her more than anything."

Lia didn't wait for a response from either of us. Instead, she backed away from the door.

"Don't trust the people in your circle," she warned before getting back in the car she arrived in.

"This shit really happening, man." Cross sighed while closing the door. "And what the fuck she talking about, with the don't trust our circle shit?"

I remembered I never got around to tell Cross that she's the one who put me on to Trey.

"She the one who told me about Trey. She probably thinks I didn't take heed to her warning and reiterating that he couldn't be trusted."

Cross looked at me oddly.

"How the fuck she knew?"

"Damn if I know. But yo, let's focus on figuring all this shit out. I would run out and get baby shit for you, but your ass will probably go crazy if she wakes up screaming."

"Take us with you," Cross pleaded, half-jokingly.

"Get her and the car seat, clown. We can talk about what the fuck you gonna do on the way to Babies "R" Us."

"Fuck would I do without you?"

"I'll be in the car," I told him before opening the door and walking out.

CHAPTER THIRTEEN

Quest

I've always heard people saying life changes in a blink of an eye, but I never paid much attention to that shit until it happened to me. Literally, one minute, things were one way, and the next minute, they were the next. Still couldn't shake the fact that my right hand, was my ex's baby father. That shit is still the punchline of jokes between me and Cross that I gotta pretend don't make me uncomfortable. However, Cross wasn't the only one with a change in his family dynamic. If niggas would have told me a thirteen-year-old would come into my life and completely shake shit up, I would have called them a liar. Not because I didn't like kids or because I didn't want any of my own, because I did. But because teenagers come with personality. They're set in their ways and for the most part, they always come with the 'you not my mother, you not my father' type mentality. Shit was different with Milani. The kid had wild respect for me and Aubri. She never made me feel as if I wasn't a parental figure in her life, or even that I was. She just respected me as the man who loved her biological mother, and would be a constant in her life. That was good enough for me. Shit, it was great. I didn't have to pretend to want her around because she made it easy to love her presence. After the Trey shit, I really had to light fire under Aubri's ass for us to move into a new spot. It was probably wrong, but I even used Milani to make her put a move on it. Since she had been staying over on weekends and shit, all I had to do was mention her safety, and Aubri was ready to move without packing her shit. She still had the apartment she had when we first met, but never went there. I thought she'd use it when she got mad at me or some shit, but she was truly one of those 'if we mad with each other, talk and get over it' type of chicks, and I loved that about her.

"What you over there day dreaming about?" Milani asked as I slid into the passenger seat of my car.

Pulling myself away from my thoughts, I looked over at her and smiled. "You killed it today, kiddo."

"Thank you, thank you. I try."

Milani had ended up going out for the basketball team and made it. I haven't missed a game yet, and didn't plan on it. Aubri usually didn't either, but she had a house showing that she couldn't reschedule, so it was just me today.

"How you feeling about this season so far?" I asked just to have something to converse about before I threw out some questions I needed her thoughts and opinions on.

"I feel like we'll make the playoffs with the way we're going. The team is solid."

"Yeah, the coach don't play and you be out there balling," I complimented her to butter her up, but it was also facts.

"Yeah, call me young Monica Wright," Milani joked.

"Would you someday want siblings?" I asked Milani, switching gears.

"I'd love that! Is Mo- I mean Aubri, pregnant?" she asked, clearly excited about the possibility, shocking me.

I thought she'd at least feel some type of way.

"She's not, but the thought of a family has been on my mind heavily. Especially since you came into our lives. I feel like a baby boy would make our little family complete."

"You consider me family?" Milani asked, surprised.

"Of course I do. With you around, I feel like I'm trying my hand at this parenting shit and I'm enjoying it," I answered honestly.

"Wow! You're the best, honestly. I enjoy the time I spend with you and Aubri. You'd think you guys had years of experience," Milani said, making me feel this feeling in my chest I've never felt before.

"I appreciate it, kiddo, but it helps that we've encountered an amazing thirteen-year-old," I let her know, winking at her.

"Quest, you don't gotta butter me up to ask me stuff." She laughed. "We still getting to know each other and all that, so I expect you to have questions for me. I have some for you.

"Oh, do you? Aight, shoot ya shot."

"Why did you guys move from the house I came to my first time coming around?" Milani asked, making me think of a way to dance around the real reason.

"It was a safer neighborhood. You down for some ice cream?" I asked, changing the subject.

"Yes!" Milani exclaimed.

The little smirk laugh she gave me after, told me she knew something else was up, but she didn't pry.

"We got a few hours 'til I gotta have you home. So, ice cream and what else?"

"Can we hit the park and play ball?"

"Oh, when she low-key trying to embarrass you 'cause she know you old and your knees ain't the same."

Milani erupted in that contagious ass laugh that reminded me of Aubri.

"Say less, though. We'll go grab ice cream and hit the court, then go scoop Aubri from work."

"That works for me."

Ashlynn

As soon as we walked through the door, CJ took off running to find his father. Although I had to face him too, I just wasn't that excited. Their chatter could be heard from the living room. Figuring it was best to get it over with sooner rather than later, I headed in there. Cross was leaning back on the couch with CJ on his lap. On the floor by his foot was the baby, in a mamaRoo rocker. The experience I went through was weird; it was like my heart sank to the bottom of my stomach, but at the same time, it fluttered. She was a baby, and babies had that effect on people.

"She's so cute," I cooed over her.

She looked nothing like my son, but she was cute nonetheless.

"CJ, go put on some comfortable clothes, then you can come tell your dad about your vacation."

CJ pouted before jumping off Christian's lap and running upstairs. For a minute, we sat there in silence. I just wanted to get everything over with. Had me feeling like I needed to just rip the Band-Aid off and move on with my life.

"Has she been this quiet the whole time I was away?" I asked him, breaking the silence.

"Hell no. She's a screamer. But Quest picked her up that swing shit and she loves it."

I hummed and nodded.

"Look, CJ and I been back from Universal for a few days, but I had us staying at a hotel while I got my thoughts together. Didn't have the chance in Universal because that little boy had me ripping and running from the moment we landed, so the time to think was much needed."

"Yeah, I understand."

"This is a hard ass pill for me to swallow, Christian. You have no idea. It's kind of worse than the act of you and Lia sleeping together. She's a baby. One, that at least for the time being, has to live in our home."

"Ash, I know, and it seems like all I have been offering you lately is apologies. I know you tired of hearing it, but I am sorry."

"Yeah, I know that. I know you didn't expect a baby to come out of this, Cross. It's just so much to deal with right now. Then we have to sit CJ down and explain to him that he has a sister and it's a lot. But I love you, and I know that loving you means that I love and accept every part of you. I can accept her. I can learn to love her, but it's going to be hard for me. I'm not mad or angry at all. I spent enough time being mad at you having sex with Lia in the first place. I'm just really hurt. Like, my husband fathered this beautiful baby girl with another woman. But as always, I guess we'll figure it out, right?"

"Is that really what you want?"

Before responding, I had to really think about what he was asking me.

"I mean, once again, I'm put in a situation where the decision was made for me. I don't have a choice in this."

"See, that's the thing. This time you do, Ash. I saw what the incident with me and Lia did to you initially, and told you I never wanted you back in that space. So yeah, you do have a choice. I'm not forcing this on you."

"You'd let me leave if I wanted to?"

"If it meant that you'd go on being the girl with the pep in your step, and the smile that lights up a room, yeah. I love you enough to let you go, even if it means sacrificing my happiness for yours."

Inhaling deeply, as if I was ingesting what he said and processing it, I wanted to say that I could overlook him having a baby and move on with my life, but I wasn't sure that I could. I was sure that I loved my family so I would fight for that.

"We'll figure it out. Has Lia reached out to you?"

"Nah. Well, she came back a little after you left, just to drop Raelynn's stuff off. Like her birth certificate and shit."

"Hmm, Raelynn. That's cute. Well, if she shows her face, we'll lay down some ground rules or whatever, but right now, we'll take it one day at a time."

"You know there's a part of me screaming on the inside that I need you and wouldn't be able to do this shit without you, right?"

Before I could reply to what he said, Raelynn started fussing. He went to get her but I stopped him. I guess my one day at a time started that moment. I put her blanket against me then picked her up. Slowly, I rocked her to calm her.

"And yes. It was written all over your face when I walked in. One day at a time though, Christian."

He offered me a weak smile and said, "One day at a time, Ashy."

Raelynn was sleeping soundly just like that, so I put her back in her mamaRoo.

"Oh, before I left, I had this weird feeling that someone was following me or watching me. I could just be being paranoid or whatever. But now we have a little baby in the house, so I'd figure it's better to let you know."

"Should have been told me, Ash. Don't worry though. I'll give you a clean piece to keep on you at all times. Just make sure you keep up going to the range, in case you ever have to use it."

"I will, Christian. I'm exhausted, though. Gonna shower and lie down."

Getting up from my seat, I ran my fingers along the side of Raelynn's rocker before heading toward the stairs.

"Ashlynn, I love you," Christian yelled out to me.

I don't think he knew how much I loved him too. Hopefully it was showing in my actions. *One day at a time,* I had to remind myself before yelling back, "I love you too."

Once I made it into my bedroom, I decided to shoot Aubri a text before heading to shower. I hadn't checked in with her, even though she'd been reaching out to me the entire time I was away.

I'm home, Aubs. Sorry I haven't returned any of your text or calls; just needed some time to process this shit. But, we'll get up soon. Like

I told Cross, I'm going to take everything one day at a time. For now though, I'ma shower and crash. Talk to you when I rise. <3

CHAPTER FOURTEEN

Aubri

Tiptoeing around the bedroom, I slipped the hoodie over my head while trying to find my phone. The room was dimly lit by the sun that was threatening to peek over the horizon. It was a little after six in the morning, and if I wanted to make it to where I was supposed to meet Ashlynn on time, I had to put a move on it.

"Fuck," I groaned under my breath after bumping into the nightstand while attempting to grab my phone.

Quest stirred, causing me to freeze where I stood. The last thing I needed was for him to wake up, questioning me about where I was going. Once I felt he was soundly back asleep, I slipped my phone in my front pocket and made my way toward the door.

"So, this what we doing now?" Quest spoke from behind me, taking me by surprise. His voice was clear as if he had been up for a while.

"What are you talking about?" I was sure to keep my tone even. He had a way of telling when something was off by the way I spoke and my body language.

"I listened to you creep around the room for a good twenty minutes. Since when we gotta creep around each other, Aub? Fuck is going on with you? This shit been going on for a minute, at that. I wasn't going to say anything 'cuz I figured you were just having some you time downstairs or some shit, but last night I went to check and you weren't there. So, again, this is what we doing now?"

"I've been taking morning runs. Why would I creep out at six and be back by the time you wake up if I'm supposedly creeping?"

"Why you taking runs this early in the morning? Especially without tell me."

"Quest, I didn't want to wake you. You already have late nights and early mornings. I'm good. Since Ashlynn been home, she's been stressed. You know she became a mom for the second time overnight. It hasn't been easy for her. We run just to catch up and for her to clear her head, that's all. Go back to sleep. I love you."

I reached for the doorknob.

"Aubri, don't lie to me again. Where you going? Where have you been going?"

"Quest, not that I should have to go this route, but if you don't believe what's going on, call Cross. He knows Ash and I been running."

Quest thought about it. I already knew he wasn't going to call Cross because of the time and it wasn't an emergency, but I also knew if he did call, Cross would corroborate the story. I didn't feel bad telling him that because it wasn't a lie. It just wasn't the whole truth. When Ashlynn and CJ came back from Universal, she did take the time she needed to work on her family and figuring things out now that Raelynn was in the picture. It wasn't easy for her though, and it still wasn't. She had taken some time off work to mother Raelynn since Quest and Cross still had to tend to business in the street, and gave me time off to be there to help her. She started taking the runs on her own, but couldn't shake the feeling of being followed, so I started joining her. It probably was stupid not to put the guys on, but they had a lot on their plates as is, and we were big girls who knew how to use a gun if necessary. Ashlynn had told Cross about it once but failed to mention that it happened again. After running with her twice, we did notice someone following us. That's when we put a plan into motion to catch the person so that Quest and Cross could handle them accordingly. If we told them now, we barely had anything to tell them besides it was a person in a black Acura with dark tint. We needed more to find the person's identity, and that's what today's run was for.

"Aight, yo. You got your piece on you?"

Cross had mentioned to Quest that he gave Ashlynn a gun, so Quest went out and copped me one too. I patted my hip to let him know that I did.

"I love you!" I yelled over my shoulder while making a break for it.

I had walked past Milani's room and thought about popping my head in to peek at her. It's something I've done every night since she had started spending the night over mmy and Quest's house. Quest's little interrogation put me behind schedule, so I skipped the routine check-in and headed downstairs and out the door. With my hands in the pocket of my hoodie, I took off running. I only ran in case Quest decided to look out the window. When I got far enough away from the house, my treads slowed until I was walking. The meeting point for Ashlynn and I was five blocks away from where I lived with Quest. It was the halfway point between our homes.

"You're late," she griped as I approached where she stood leaning against the lamppost.

"Got caught by Quest."

"And you still made it out?" She chuckled.

"Yeah. I told him the truth, just not the whole truth. It worked. I'm sure he's going to ask Cross later when they link up, have we been running. But you ready?"

I could sense the hesitation coming from Ashlynn, but today wasn't the day for her to have doubts.

"I mean. Yeah, I guess. You sure we can pull this off, right?"

"It's not rocket science, Ash. All we going to do is let whoever it is follow us. Take a few pictures, make sure we get the plate, and show Quest and Cross. They will handle the rest."

I walked away toward the car, Ashland begged one of the young boys that worked for Quest and Cross to secure for us. We couldn't take one of our cars because if caught, Quest and Cross would question why we needed a car on a 'run.' We had parked the car yesterday morning, so we didn't have to worry about going to get it today or whatever. All we had to do was get in drive around, and let who ever follow us like they'd been doing. I don't know why Ashlynn was acting like I was asking her to kill someone's grandmother. Waiting for her to find the courage to go through with it could have possibly taken all morning. We didn't have that type of time. Hopefully, me walking away was enough to push her forward. As I approached the car, I glanced over my shoulder and there she was. Tailing a little behind, but following, nonetheless.

"Lord, cover us," Ash whispered as she jerked open the passenger door.

"We good."

Slamming the door, as I sat in the driver's seat, I grabbed at the seatbelt and pulled it over me.

Click, Clack

The sound of a gun cocking back froze Ashlynn and me in our seats. My eyes shifted toward the rear-view mirror and that's when they met his. His were blank as they stared back at me through the mirror. His hand was steady as he held the cold steel to the back of my head. My eyes shifted in the direction of Ashlynn. Through my peripheral, I could see her inching for the gun that was tucked beneath her sweater.

"I must admit. The both of you are much smarter than I thought. You made one mishap and that mishap is going to cost you your life. If you knew someone was following you, why wouldn't you assume that I saw when y'all parked this car yesterday?"

Although panic was setting in, I had to wear a poker face. This is a risk I willingly took when Ashlynn and I came up with the plan. There was no point in freaking out now, not when he literally held my life in his hand.

Nudging the gun against the back of my head, he taunted me.

"Nothing to say now?"

"Do it," I taunted back.

"What fun is that?" he laughed.

Ashlynn was eerily silent, causing my eyes to shift in her direction again. Her body was stiff as a board but because I was staring at her, I could see her hand still sliding toward her side. If I saw it, that meant he could see it too.

"I wouldn't…"

He went to speak, but in the time he took his attention off Ashlynn, she had her gun drawn and aimed at his face.

"You're quick." He chuckled.

The fact that he was completely unbothered by the gun in his face scared me. But still, I didn't show it. My attention zoomed in on how Ashlynn's hand shook nervously, as her finger rested on the trigger. I was beginning to worry that he would let off a shot and spill my brains all over the car, before she could catch her bearings and pull the trigger. We've practiced. We've taken trips to the gun range for situations exactly like this; but still, she was nervous.

"You might want to put the gun down, Ashlynn. If you shoot me, y'all will never see her…"

His head turned in my direction before he completed his sentence. That was all the distraction Ashlynn needed to let off her shot.

Pop!

A shrieked escaped Ashlynn's mouth as if she wasn't the one who pulled the trigger. I turned slightly to find him slumped over between my seat and the back seat.

"Get out," I barked.

Ashlynn's hands shook violently as she stared blankly at his dead body.

"Ashlynn, get a grip and get out the car!"

I huffed while wiping down anything that we could have possibly touched. We both wore gloves, but my nerves wouldn't allow me to get out the car without wiping it down. We wore gloves without even knowing things would turn deadly, but luckily, we did.

"I. I – Killed him," Ashlynn stuttered as we ran away from the car. I didn't even know who he was. But something told me Ashlynn did.

Suddenly, I stopped in my tracks as something hit me like a ton of bricks.

If you shoot me, y'all will never see her... I heard his voice over and over as I fumbled for my phone.

"Pick up the phone. Pick up the phone. Pick up the fucking..."

"Fuck you screaming for. What happened?" Quest finally answered.

"Go check on Milani," I instructed him.

"You know she not getting up 'til like ten. It's Saturday. I don't wanna deal with no moody ass—"

"Quest! Go check on her, please," my voice cracked as my panic reached an all-time high.

He sighed, but I could hear him fumbling as he got out of the bed.

"Quest, hurry up!"

"Aubri, calm down, damn. Can I put some fucking shorts on?"

I knew Quest liked to sleeping butt ass naked, but I needed him to move a little faster.

"After you check on Mi…"

"Yo. Milani," Quest called out. "Milani! Aub, she's not here, yo."

"What you mean she not there?" My heart dropped to the pit of my stomach.

"I'm fucking with you. She in here reading a book."

A wave of relief overcame me hearing that she was fine. I couldn't even put energy into being pissed at Quest for playing because we had a dead body a few feet away from us.

"Bae… I, I gotta tell you something."

"What happened, Aubri?" His tone went flat due to how serious I sounded. "Wait, hold on."

"Quest!" I tried to stop him before he put me on hold but it was too late.

I looked back at Ashlynn who was standing with her arms wrapped around her, rocking back and forth. The silencer of the gun was peeking out of her hoodie pocket. After taking two steps in her direction, I was in her space. Gently, I grabbed at her arm and pulled her. We needed to put some distance between us and the car.

"Aub. Where y'all at?"

"Can you please listen to me?"

"Shut the fuck up, Aubri. Where y'all at? Come home now!" he barked.

The tone of his voice shook my body at its core. I've heard Quest angry, but never has he used that tone with me. Here I was risking my life for him and his friend, and he was yelling at me like I was a child.

"Aubri. There was an explosion."

"Wha, what you mean there was an explosion?"

"You and Ash, gotta… Yo, just come on. You just gotta get here now. I can't believe this shit."

"You're scaring me, Quest. What happened?"

"Cross…"

Hearing the pain in his voice as he said Cross's name ripped at my heart. Slowly, I hung up the phone and turned to Ashlynn.

"There's been an explosion and Cross… We just have to hurry up."

"No. No."

Her body jerked and fell into mine. She shuddered before sobbing.

"We don't know what happened, Ash. We gotta get out of here."

"He said we'll never see her," Ashlynn muttered.

Ashlynn

Aubri yanked at my arm, pulling me in the opposite direction of the car we were abandoning with the body of the man I just killed left inside.

"Snap out of this shit, Ash," she barked.

My legs were moving with no help from me. The strength of Aubri's tugs were guiding me in the direction I needed to go. My mind raced from thoughts of Cross, CJ, and Raelynn, to me possibly going to jail. Jail didn't even sound as bad as losing the people who made life worth living. What would I do without my husband and son? All I could think was his threat to not see her. Milani was accounted for. Could the her have been Raelynn? She wasn't my child and I was still coming to terms of her being a part of my family, but I definitely didn't want her harmed.

"I can't do this." Suddenly, I stopped and heaved. I glanced back, although we were about four blocks away from the incident. Leaning over, I placed my hands on my knees, and inhaled and exhaled rapidly. My hands shook unsteadily as I stood up, frantically checking our surroundings.

"Listen to me, Ashlynn. You must pull it together. We have to get home and find out what's going on. Push what happened back there to the back of your mind. You hear me?"

"What do I do if something... Something horrible. What am I

supposed to do?!" I wailed at the top of my lungs.

Aubri walked away from me, closer to the corner. She stuck her hand out in an attempt to flag down a cab. A minute had passed at a snail's pace when finally, a cab pulled up curbside. She opened the back door and held it open, waiting for me to get in. When I did, she slid in behind me before rambling off her address.

"No, I need to go home," I found the words to say.

She shook her head no.

"What do you mean no? My husband, my son, Aubri. Take me to—"

Aubri's head snapped in my direction. "I said no! You want answers, so do I, and we will get them, but Quest said to come home so that's where we're going. Please, okay. I'm on edge too, Ashlynn. No, it's not my husband or my children, but you all are my fucking family. You not in this alone. Let's just get to Quest."

Responding crossed my mind, but the words wouldn't come. She was right in a sense. I knew Quest and knew that he would do whatever, whenever it was necessary for his family and mine, so if he instructed us to go to him first, it was for good reason, but even with knowing that, it didn't put me at ease. I just needed to know that they were alive.

"My son, my life is on the line here," I whispered, hoping Aubri would feel my pain.

She looked over at me and the look on her face told me she did. She reached her arm around me and pulled me into her.

"Everything will be okay. We have to believe that."

"How did this happen? How did we get here?" I cried onto Aubri's shoulder.

My questions went unanswered as I knew they would. Even if she knew what to say to me, the words would never be spoken in the back of a cab. My stomach was in knots and my heart was aching. I just needed to speak to Cross, needed to hear CJ and Raelynn's voices. I needed to know that they were okay.

The cab came to a stop outside the gates of Aubri and Quest's home, but I couldn't move. I wanted answers. We were at the place where I could get them, yet, I couldn't move. Looking over at Aubri, she was doing something on her phone.

"One sec," she instructed the driver.

Not even a minute later, Milani came jogging down the long driveway, out of the gates, and over to where we were in the cab. She waited at the passenger window until the driver rolled it down. She handed him a bill and told him to keep the change. It's like Aubri knew I wouldn't be able to move on my own. When she opened the door to get out, she grabbed my hand and pulled me out behind her.

My legs were jelly beneath me and threatened to betray me. Each step became a little harder to take. Each breath I took became a little harder to inhale.

"I can't breathe, Aubs." I felt as if I was suffocating, but we were out in the open.

"What can I get for her?" Milani asked with a worried and pained expression on her face.

"It's okay, Milani. Go inside. I got her."

Aubri waited for Milani to disappear back into the house before turning to me.

"Slow breaths, Ash," she coached me.

Slowly, I inhaled and exhaled, feeling as if I was releasing what little life was in me.

"I just need to hear their voices. I need to know that they are okay."

"And we will find out. We just have to go into the house."

Shrugging her off, I looked toward the house, and after willing myself to put one foot in front of the other, I made my way toward the door.

"It's been damn near an hour. I told you to fucking find them or any information that will lead me to them. What the fuck am I paying you for, huh?"

We entered the house to find Quest barking on someone. As expected, he was on his job, trying to get information. Still, I wasn't at ease.

"Call you back when you got what I asked for."

He hung up so fast that I was sure the other person wasn't able to answer. His reason for hanging up wasn't clear until he turned around and greeted us with sad eyes. His call ended abruptly because we had arrived. Maybe he was going to give us the answers Aubri assured me I'd get.

"Quest, what's going on?" My tone was uneasy but I got my sentence out.

"Sit down." His request came across as more of a demand, so although I wanted to object and for him to get on with telling me what I wanted to know, I sat. "There was an explosion at the crib." His voiced cracked as if he was about to break down. I knew Quest was trying to hold it together for me; it was written all over his face. "They haven't found any bodies, but the fire department is still going through the wreckage. Quavo was doing his routine drive by when he came up on the scene and asked questions. He's who called me."

Quest paused and looked over at Aubri. "He's on his way to take Milani home. We'll be busy."

She nodded and continued running her hand up and down my back.

"Quest, Quavo is coming up," the voice boomed through the intercom system they had wired through the house. It was Bo, Quest's morning shift security.

Quest walked over to the intercom on the living room wall, pressed a button, and spoke, "Good looking, Bo."

Leaving us in the living room, Quest headed to the front door to let Quavo in. Moments later, they joined us.

"Ash, I'm sorry, sis. We definitely going to find them; well."

Quest added, "Cross is smart. Crafty. We gotta know he would do whatever to keep him and the kids alive."

"Milani!" Aubri called out.

Footsteps could be heard nearing us.

"Yes. I was in the kitchen finishing my food."

"Are you done?" Aubri asked her without taking her eyes off of Quest.

"Yep."

"Okay. Quavo is going to take you home. I hate that our weekend has to end abruptly but…"

"I understand," Milani interrupted her.

Aubri stood up, walked around the couch, and pulled Milani into her. She took a deep breath; I could tell by the way her shoulders rose. "I'll call you as soon as I hear something."

"They good, Aunt Ash." She blew me a kiss, that I slowly reached out to catch, and placed my hand across my heart.

"Quavo, can you please let Quest know as soon as you drop her off?" Aubri asked.

"Of course," Quavo stated before following Milani toward the front door.

The room fell silent; it was draining. We looked around at each other eerily, each afraid to say what we all were thinking. If there was an explosion at the house where I left my family sleeping, it only meant one thing: none of us wanted to face the fact that…

"They might be dead," I whispered before my shoulders shuddered and I fell backward, slumping into the couch. Admitting what could be a fact out loud, had me feeling as if my world had collapsed, and slowly, I was falling into the sunken place.

Again, the room was silent. This time, instead of being interrupted by words none of us wanted to hear, it was interrupted by the sound of Quest's phone ringing. Well, the phone barely had a chance to ring because after a half of a ring, he answered.

"Who is this?"

The look of relief on Quest's face, told me that it was Cross. A little at ease, but not completely.

"Where are you? On the way."

He hung up and gestured for us to follow him.

"Where is he?" I asked as we walked out the front door.

All Quest said was, "The hospital."

"Are they all okay? CJ and Raelynn with him, right? Are they hurt?"

He turned around as we approached his Range. "Ashlynn, please, sis. Let's get there."

Solemnly, I pulled open the back door and climbed in the jeep. Aubri got in the passenger's seat and Cross got in the driver's.

"Wait," Aubri spoke right before Quest pulled off.

She undid her seatbelt, climbed out the car, and joined me in the back. I slid closer to her, leaning over, and resting my head in her lap. She played in my hair, as her legs gently bounced up and down.

"They are fine," she whispered to me over and over.

Cross

You know when you can hear people talking? Yelling? Saying your name? But you don't actually hear them? I probably was losing my mind, but that's sort of what I was experiencing. Sitting in the emergency room covered, in a mixture of blood and debris had my mind fried. People around me were chatting it up, the ER was busy, people coming and going, but I heard nothing. Faintly, I could hear someone calling out for me, but the sound wasn't strong enough to fully get my attention. I was there, but somewhere else at the same time.

"Mom!" That got my attention. When I looked up from the daze I was in, I spotted CJ flying into his Ashlynn's arms.

She dropped to her knees and pulled him into her. Together they cried.

"Are you okay? You hurt, CJ?"

He shook his head no. He wasn't but I was. Beyond repair.

"I just have this cut but it's not bad. I'm a big boy. Daddy made sure I was okay," he explained to her.

My eyes wouldn't leave them. Although I knew she had questions that would lead to me divulging in things I didn't want to discuss, I couldn't force myself to look away. Not after the moments I spent wondering if I'd ever see her again. My eyes were blurry and my focus was off. Again, I didn't know if it was because of the tears that were building up, debris, or something else. Rubbing to get better focus helped a little bit.

"Bro," Quest started speaking, while occupying the seat previously held by CJ.

With my eyes on them still, I acknowledged him. "She might die. If she does, that's on me."

Silence. As expected. What could he have said to me? What in that moment would have made everything alright? Quest knew to keep the prepared, Hallmark card, sympathy bullshit to himself. Nothing would change the predicament we were in. I watched intensely as CJ stood to the side with Aubri, and Ash made her way over to me.

"I thought I lost you," Ashlynn admitted as she kneeled in front of me and rested her head against my midsection.

Yeah, I wanted to reach out for her. Wrap her in my arms and let her know that I was good, but I wasn't, so I couldn't.

"Where's Raelynn?" she asked once she realized that I wasn't going to offer her any words.

Pressing my eyes closed, I shook my head slowly, wishing her to change the subject or leave me the fuck alone. Silently, I was praying to be back in that space where there was noise but I couldn't hear what was being said. My prayers went unanswered.

"Where is Raelynn?" she repeated.

"Stop fucking asking me that shit," I exploded, jumping to my feet, pushing Ashlynn off me in the process. Guilt consumed me, but it didn't stop me from walking away from her.

"What the fuck is wrong with you?" Quest hollered as he jogged to catch up with me.

His plea went unanswered as well. I walked straight out of the emergency room and posted up against one of the glass windows.

"Christian." Quest never said my real name, so I knew he had it up to the limit with my shit, but he couldn't possibly understand how I felt. "Listen to me, bro. Whatever happens, we are all we got, my nigga. You not about to implode or blow the fuck up on the people who care about you. What the fuck happened and where is Rae?"

Staring off into space, I coughed and wiped the tears that flowed down my face. Wasn't trying to cry in front of CJ, Ashlynn, and Aubs. A few tears, aight, but I would never allow them to see me cry the way I needed to cry. It was different with Quest. My body jerked forward and a wounded cry escaped me. My brother grabbed me and pulled me into him.

"We'll get through this, Cross. On everything I love. You know I'm here for you, bro."

I heard him. I felt him, and knew his words were valid, but it wasn't enough to stop the release I needed that came in the form of breaking down. He didn't try to stop it either. He allowed me to be weak in the way that he knew I needed in that moment.

"Let that shit out. I'm right here, Cross. I got you. I got Ash and CJ too, you know that, right?"

I was starting to think that I would never have this Quest back. I mean, I never really lost my brother, but the relationship we had after the Lia shit turned into brothers just being brothers because regardless of what went down, they were brothers. The Quest that showed up right now was pre-Lia Quest. My brother was back.

"What I'ma do if she dies, bro." I dry heaved while trying to catch my breath.

"You got her here, Cross. You did your part. We gotta pray those doctors do their thing and keep Rae here with us."

I shook my head frantically.

"I had to make a choice, bro. I didn't even think or hesitate. I mean, I care about baby girl. You know?"

He was confused and it was obvious.

"Cops told me it was a gas leak," I started to explain. "It wasn't. CJ and I was in the kitchen because he woke up early as fuck. Trying to make him breakfast and shit, but something wasn't sitting right with me. Checked the security footage and seen niggas in the back. First instinct was to get CJ out the crib. So, I took him through the front and put him in the car, told him to stay down and shit. Turned to go back in for my gun and shit, one bomb went off on one side of the house and that was the moment I thought about getting Raelynn. I made it to her, but on our way out, another one went off and..."

Another breakdown was nearing.

"Barely made out but she got burned bad, man. All because I made the choice to get CJ out first. If she dies, it's on me."

"Cross, this shit ain't your fault. How the fuck were you supposed to know they were on that type time. You didn't, and when you did, you tried to… you did get her. This ain't on you, and she gonna be aight."

"I don't know. I mean, it probably make sense. You know I don't really feel that father, daughter type bond with Raelynn how I feel with CJ, and I didn't understand why, because I do care about her. And of course, I don't want her to die, Q. But, she not even mine and maybe deep down I knew that so I didn't bother getting to her first."

"That's not even you, Cross. If Milani was at your crib this weekend, you would have went for her even though she not blood related to you. So, feeling like she wasn't yours had nothing to do with this. You were dealt a shitty ass hand this morning, man, and you played it the best way you could. Don't beat yourself up over this. She gonna be aight."

"I just need to clear my head. I can't even start to explain this shit to Ash."

"Just do what you do best, bro. Assure her that everything will be aight."

Was everything going to be aight, though?

"Yo, what you mean she not yours?"

Sighing, I ran my hands over my head and down my face.

"They wanted to have some blood on deck for her surgery in case she needed a transfusion. I jumped at the opportunity to donate my shit. They told me I couldn't after going through her file and shit. You know this the hospital she was born at so they had everything on her. But the doctor pulled me to the side and told me I couldn't possibly be her father. She's type O, I'm A, and her file says Lia is—"

"AB, right? Remember Li's car accident a while back? I gave her blood."

"Yeah. So, basically, after all that doctor lingo, it came down to type AB and type A not being able to birth a Type O child."

"Aight, look. Let's not even get into her paternity right now, bro. You been taking care of her since Lia dipped. Accepted her into your family; we all did. So regardless of all that, we need to be in there when she comes out of surgery. Right now, that's all that matters. And as soon as we get an update on her condition, we move on to finding out who the fuck is responsible for this. Family first."

"Always," I told him, before pulling myself together and heading back inside with Quest on my heels. "I'm sorry, Ash."

She shrugged. "What's going on with—"

"Family of Raelynn Perkins."

Immediately, I turned to be greeted by the same doctor that told me Raelynn wasn't my daughter.

"How is she?" Ashlynn probed.

"She's out of surgery. It went well. Healing will be an uphill battle, but she will make a full recovery. No major damage, and thanks to the amazing plastic surgeon we have on our team, she will have minimal scarring."

"Surgery? What?" Ashlynn looked back at me before turning her attention back to the doctor. "Can we see her?"

"Of course, just the parents."

Quest wrapped his arm around CJ's shoulder and pulled him

closer to him.

"We got CJ. We'll be right here," Quest told me.

Ashlynn and I both hugged CJ before following the doctor to Raelynn's room.

CHAPTER FIFTEEN

Aubri

After a week in the hospital, Raelynn was finally getting back to being herself. They weren't ready to discharge her yet, but she was able to go to the play room in the pediatric ward now for some much-needed playtime. There wasn't much she could do since she was still little, usually we read to her. That's where Ashlynn and I were now, with her. Not only had it been a week since someone attempted to kill Cross and Raelynn, but also since Ashlynn and I mentioned what went down. Every day, I wanted to tell Quest what happened, but Ashlynn helped me see that the time wasn't right. Our focus was on helping Raelynn through recovery and having as much of a normal childhood as possible. It took a village. While I was here with Ash and Raelynn, the guys were out grabbing lunch. They knew to be back in an hour when Raelynn would be heading back to her room.

"Ash, how are you feeling?" We were sitting on the floor showing Raelynn pictures in the book *Don't let the pigeon drive the bus*. Ash looked up briefly from what she was doing and gave me a weak smile.

"You know, I'm okay. I'm happy baby girl is recovering. It's still surreal to me. Became a stepmother overnight, and almost lost my entire family right after. It's a lot, Aubs, but I'm hanging in there and just looking forward to putting this all behind us. Once Raelynn is home, we can tell the guys about..."

"Yeah. Everything will work out."

"What am I supposed to do if Lia comes back? How do I give this precious little baby, whom I've grown to really care about, back to her? Sometimes I wish Cross didn't tell me that he wasn't her father. If Lia would have come back when I thought she was his, probably wouldn't have hesitated to let her go and work out some blended family thing. But now, after almost losing this baby doll, I wouldn't want to give her back to Lia. What do I do now?"

Leaning my head on Ashlynn's shoulder, I reached over and gently tickled Raelynn. "You fight tooth and nail. Your egg or his sperm wasn't used to create her, but you and Cross are her parents; Lia left her. Biology does not determine that. We'll fight tooth and nail."

She smiled and lifted Raelynn up. "What would we do without Aubs? Huh, Rae?"

"How'd she do today?" the pediatric nurse asked as she joined Ashlynn and me.

We looked up at her. Her presence meant playtime was over.

"Better than yesterday. Little baby is feeling good. She didn't cry and wasn't trying to pick at her scab."

"That's great news. The guys are back and waiting in her room."

We got up off the floor. Ashlynn handed Raelynn over to the

nurse, who had to transport Raelynn back to her room. Together, we headed back to the other wing of the pediatric floor.

"Look who's back," the Nurse announced as we walked into her room.

I took a seat on Quest's lap and watched as the nurse gave Rae a quick examination before leaving.

"Was she fussy and shit?" Cross asked.

"Nope. Today was a good day. What did you bring me to eat?"

We all laughed at Ashlynn's focus switching right to food. Shoot, the same thing was on my mind, but before I could speak up on it, my phone started ringing. The number was a New York area code but wasn't saved to my phone. Usually, unknown numbers went to voicemail, but I decided to answer.

"Hello."

"Fortunately for me, Ashlynn has a horrible shot. Unfortunate for you, though. I hear baby Raelynn survived. Hope Milani is that lucky. Junior High School 113, right?" Slowly, I pulled the phone away from my ear, looking at it oddly. Sluggishly, I released the hold I had on my phone and allowed it to crash to the floor. The entire room fell silent and all eyes shifted to me.

"Gi—Give me your gun," I instructed Quest.

"What? Who was that?"

Slowly, I rose to my feet while reaching for Quest's waist. He gripped my wrist and pushed it away from him.

"What the fuck is wrong with you, Aubs? Who was on the phone?"

I turned to Ashlynn with glassy eyes.

"He's alive." Quickly, I glanced down at my watch. "I have to get to Milani before she gets out of school." With that said, I was gone. No explanation, no nothing. Only thing on my mind was getting to my daughter. I let her down before, and since she's been in my life, I made a vow to her that I'd never do it again. If he wanted her, he had to kill me first.

Once outside the hospital, it was easy for me to hail a cab. They were always circling the area since it was a hotspot for people who needed them.

"Adelphi, between DeKalb and Lafayette."

I couldn't stop fidgeting. My palms were getting clammy and my heart rate quickened. I had to get to Milani in time. Again, I looked at my watch. I had exactly twenty minutes to get to her school before she would be let out.

"Please, a little faster. It's an emergency at my daughter's school."

The driver didn't hesitate to go a little faster while still abiding by traffic laws. I wanted to pull his ass out of the car and take over driving myself, but I had to remain calm. Ten minutes before the bell would ring letting her out, and I was just a few blocks away. With traffic, I'd be there in fifteen. That wasn't good enough for me. Reaching down in my bag, I pulled out a fifty-dollar bill, tossed it over into the front seat, and demanded he let me out right there. Once my feet hit the pavement, I took off running.

Panting, and barely able to catch my breath, I leaned over the railing at her school's entrance. I felt around my purse and pockets until I remembered I dropped my phone back at the hospital.

"Fuck!" I had no way of contacting Milani and wouldn't be able to find her once the sea of kids was released. I had to get to her before she left the building.

Quickly, I pulled open the door to the entrance, went through the proper channels of signing in before heading straight to the office. I was able to speak with the assistant principal who called Milani down to the office over the loudspeaker.

"Thank you so much," I thanked her before taking my seat to wait.

My leg shook as I tapped the tips of my nails against each other. My nerves didn't settle until Milani came walking through the office door, just as the bell sounded letting the kids out. Even after seeing her there and well, I was still nervous.

"What's up? Everything okay?"

Hugging her tightly, I whispered, "Yes, I just really wanted to see you."

I hated lying to her, but I didn't need her nervous and scared. Not until I got her somewhere safe.

"Oh, you should have texted. My cousin came into town today and he was picking me up. I would have told him I'd see him after I hung out with you."

"I was in the neighborhood so it was random. Where are you supposed to meet him?" I asked as we walked out of the office.

"Right out front."

"Okay, let's go."

Although we were walking through her school, I couldn't help but look over my shoulders ever so often. I didn't know how long his reach was and who he knew. An attack on Milani and me could come from anywhere. I had to be on point.

"You see him?" I asked her once we got outside.

She tiptoed and looked around the group of people who were outside of the school.

"Nah."

I watched as she pulled out her phone and tapped on the screen.

"He's walking from the train station," she told me.

Okay, waiting a few minutes wouldn't hurt. She was with me. No matter what happened, I'd make sure nothing happened to her.

"Milani, you have Quest, Cross, and Ashlynn's number, right?" I knew she did, but I couldn't be too sure.

"Yeah, of course. Quest texts me like every morning. Did you make it to school, Milani? Do you need anything?"

Even with what was going on, that made me smile. Quest tried to hide the attachment he had to Milani from me ever since he expressed wanting me to have his baby. But hearing things like that reminded me just how involved he was in her life, and how much he wanted her in his.

"Good. If anything happens—if I tell you to run, go hide, or anything like that—get somewhere safe and call them. Send a group message if you have to. One of them, if not all, will respond right away."

"Okay, but what's going on? Does this have to do with the fire at Uncle Cross's crib?"

I shook my head no. This had to do with the gangster that I decided to love and allow to love me back, and at the same time, had everything to do with the decisions I made.

"Just make sure you do that, okay? Let me see your phone."

She nodded while handing me her phone. "I will."

Heading straight for her messages, I started a text to Quest.

"I think that's him coming up the block, come on."

With my face still buried in her phone, I followed behind her to meet her cousin.

"Big babyyyyyyy," she squealed to who I assumed was her cousin. I was in the middle of wrapping up my spiel to Quest. I needed to give him instructions on where to meet Milani and me.

It wasn't until I heard, "Little baby," was I able to take my focus off the message I was sending.

That voice froze me. While the tone was full of joy being spoken to Milani, all I heard was the malice behind it. Afraid of who I would see, but still needing to be certain, I uneasily raised my head from looking down at the phone and my eyes locked with his.

"No, no. Noooo."

My head became super light and the grimace on his face was the last thing I saw before darkness.

TO BE CONTINUED

Looking for a publishing home?

Royalty Publishing House, Where the Royals reside, is accepting submissions for writers in the urban fiction genre. If you're interested, submit the first 3-4 chapters with your synopsis to submissions@royaltypublishinghouse.com.

Check out our website for more information: www.royaltypublishinghouse.com.

Text ROYALTY to 42828 to join our mailing list!

To submit a manuscript for our review, email us at
submissions@royaltypublishinghouse.com

Text RPHCHRISTIAN to 22828 for our
CHRISTIAN ROMANCE novels!

Text RPHROMANCE to 22828 for our
INTERRACIAL ROMANCE novels!

Get LiT!

Download the LiT eReader app today and enjoy exclusive content, free books, and more

Do You Like CELEBRITY GOSSIP?

Check Out QUEEN DYNASTY!
Visit Our Site: www.thequeendynasty.com

CPSIA information can be obtained
at www.ICGtesting.com
Printed in the USA
LVOW10s1330300817

546968LV00022BA/567/P